If I had expected to be the object of Simon's scrutiny, I would have dressed more carefully. As it was, my hair was pulled back in a rubber band and I was wearing last year's grubby jeans. But it was too late to do anything but hold my stomach in, so I concentrated intensely on that.

"You should always wear jeans, Brenna," Simon said, obviously mellowed by the soda.

My brother chortled. "She certainly should, seeing she's always up to her ears in the dogs' flea dip!"

I shot him a look; my ears were burning. Could it be that Simon really liked me???

Dear Readers,

We at Silhouette would like to thank all our readers for your many enthusiastic letters. In direct response to your encouragement, we are now publishing *four* FIRST LOVEs every month.

As always FIRST LOVEs are written especially for and about you—your hopes, your dreams, your ambitions.

Please continue to share your suggestions and comments with us; they play an important part in our pleasing you.

I invite you to write to us at the address below:

Nancy Jackson
Senior Editor
Silhouette Books
P.O. Box 769
New York, N.Y. 10019

PUPPY LOVE
Janice Harrell

First Love from Silhouette

Published by Silhouette Books New York

America's Publisher of Contemporary Romance

SILHOUETTE BOOKS, a Division of Simon & Schuster, Inc.
1230 Avenue of the Americas, New York, N.Y. 10020

Copyright © 1983 by Janice F. Harrell

Distributed by Pocket Books

ISBN: 0-671-53367-3

First Silhouette Books printing October, 1983

10 9 8 7 6 5 4 3 2 1

PUPPY
LOVE

That was the summer my parents continually kept asking me if I had decided on my future career yet. I don't think they had any idea how often they brought it up. Daddy took to bringing home tales of other people's daughters who, with single-minded purpose, were preparing for careers in forestry or criminal justice. And Mom was even worse. She couldn't so much as read in the newspaper about somebody swimming the English channel without looking at me speculatively, wondering whether I was channel-swimming material. It was clear that in my parents' eyes I was the only sixteen year old in the world without a fixed career goal, or as they put it, some sense of direction.

I let all their subtle hints pass over my head. I am pretty good at ignoring if I put my mind to it. And I hoped this would blow over, but instead, the campaign gathered steam. I was sitting at the breakfast table buttering a biscuit when the conversation suddenly took an all-too-predictable turn. My mother began talking about how satisfying Aunt Betty found her career in dentistry and suddenly said casually, "I wonder if Brenna might enjoy spending the summer with Betty."

"I don't think so," I said promptly.

"Betty suggested it herself, dear. The twins will be away at camp, so you don't have to worry about them."

The last time we had visited Aunt Betty and Uncle Eliot years ago, the twins had tied me to a tree and, pretending to scalp me, had cut off one of my braids with their safety scissors. But I was reasonably certain that as sophomores in high school they weren't still playing cowboys and Indians. That wasn't what was bothering me. I just didn't want to spend the summer with Aunt Betty.

Behind his newspaper my father gave an unintelligible growl which gradually became recognizable as speech. "Can't hurt your aunt's feelings, Brenna," he muttered.

I didn't like it. It was most unlike Daddy to speak at the breakfast table. This had all the marks of a conspiracy. They seemed to have already made up their minds to ship me off to Texas.

Jack gave me a sympathetic grin and announced that he'd have to be off or he'd be late. Lucky Jack. He'd had the foresight to get a summer job. Nobody was bugging him.

Jack's leaving barely caused Mom to miss a beat. "Betty was kind enough to suggest that you might like to fill in for her receptionist while she's on vacation," she went on with mounting enthusiasm. "You could earn some extra money and at the same time really get an inside view of the practice." Mom forgot that I had already had a view of the practice that time I fell into the twins' tiger pit and chipped my front tooth so that Aunt Betty had to file it down. I could still see that poster in front of the dentist's chair—an artist's conception of tooth decay germs with the jolly legend, "As soon as you stop eating food, the food starts eating your teeth." All around the office, models of teeth with pink plastic gums were silently yakking.

My biscuit grew cold in my hand as I considered how to put a stop to Mom's onslaught. The solution that occurred to me offered only temporary relief, but it had the merit of simplicity. "It's ten of eight," I said quietly.

Mom stifled an involuntary shriek and grabbed for her car keys. I knew she was planning to go to an auction in Raleigh and would need at least an hour beforehand to go over the junk with a magnifying glass. That is standard procedure for auction goers, and Mom is not the only antique dealer who rises with the sun for auctions, but I'm sure Dad is positively the only attorney for five hundred miles who thinks he has to be in the office every morning by eight. He began moving painfully towards the door, his eyes looking saggy and red like a bloodhound's. He always looks that way when he leaves in the morning. I've never seen a stronger argument for sleeping until noon.

When their cars pulled out of the driveway I turned, as I always do in moments of stress, to cleaning my guinea pig's cage. Since my parents had started this "sense of direction" thing, that guinea pig had the cleanest cage in Christendom.

Of course I could tell them that I didn't want to be a dentist and that I didn't want to visit Aunt Betty. But that would bring them back full circle to the question of what *did* I want to do.

My parents' problem, as I saw it, was that they were in the grip of their backgrounds. Mom's people were hard-working Scandinavian immigrants and Dad's were Kansas pioneers. It was inevitable that Mom and Dad would be workaholics. They couldn't help it. My problem was simply that I had been born into this hard-driving family. I wasn't cut from the same cloth. I saw myself more as a Ferdinand the Bull sort, content just to smell the flowers.

I piled a small mountain of fresh timothy hay into the cage of my guinea pig. He dived in with a happy whir, like the sound of a well-oiled machine. Nobody would say that a guinea pig is an exciting pet, but I liked watching him. He was the long-haired variety, which is to say he looked like a particularly fluffy dust mop. People who don't know about guinea pigs have mistaken him for an unusually taciturn Yorkshire terrier. After plumping up the hay, I gave him the leafy top of a celery stalk. He snatched it greedily with his mouth and began to dispatch it, the jaws of his impassive guinea pig face working quickly. *"Whrrrr,"* he murmured. I thought how nice it would be to be so happy. That's how low I was feeling. I was actually sitting there wishing I were a guinea pig.

That evening Jack made light of my problem. "For Pete's sake, Brenna," he said. "Don't over-dramatize this thing. You don't have to decide what you're going to do with the rest of your life. All you have to do is get busy. You know how much it grates on Mom and Dad for people to look like they're schlepping around doing nothing for months on end."

"It is customary, I believe," I said stiffly, "for students to take a vacation in the summer."

"Look, if you don't want my advice," he said, "don't ask for it." I couldn't remember that I had asked for it, but he went on. "Just look like you're interested in something," he said. "Take a course, refinish some furniture, start a rock collection. They won't care what it is. All they're saying is that you should look like you're going someplace and not just wasting your time."

"I have worked for this vacation," I replied

with dignity. "I have looked forward to this vacation, and I am going to enjoy this vacation."

He snorted. "Yeah, you look like you're enjoying it all right."

"Taking courses and refinishing furniture happen to be two of the things I am trying to get a vacation from this summer," I went on. "And as you well know, I am not the least bit interested in rocks."

"Okay, okay, I'm just trying to help. Do it your own way. Enjoy yourself." Jack's voice was heavy with irony.

What he didn't understand is how I had planned of doing nothing this summer. That was what I had in mind when I was sloshing through winter rain to go to school, and spending my evenings studying biology, doing algebra, and babysitting. When summer comes, I had promised myself, I will do absolutely nothing. Nothing. I had spent a good part of my babysitting money on some dresses that would be perfect to do nothing in.

Also, there was the possibility that a summer romance might materialize. Dancing in the moonlight, long walks, shared banana splits—I hadn't worked out all the details yet. I was willing to let things develop, but the general tone of the thing was clear. It was to be fun, fun, fun. I didn't think it would be too difficult to manage a summer romance because I wasn't at all particular. After all, I didn't need true love. What I needed, if I may risk repeating myself, was *fun*.

Of course when I had planned this long, slow summer of leisure, I hadn't realized that the sight of me doing nothing was going to drive my parents off the rails and result in their showering on me with a hail of suggestions about how to give meaning and purpose to my life. It was a problem. But I had no intention of letting them stampede me into refinishing furniture. In my own quiet way I can be very determined. Rest, relaxation, fun—that was the kind of summer I wanted, and I was determined to get it if it killed me.

Nothing more was said about Aunt Betty or careers that night because Jack's friend, Simon, came over to play chess and I took the precaution of stationing myself by the chess board and watching with rapt attention. Luckily, neither Jack nor Simon is the sort of high-strung person who is driven crazy by rapt attention.

Usually their games are long, quiet, and deeply boring. But tonight Simon was off his game. In a surprisingly short time Jack called, "Check," and chortled, "you walked right into that, Simon, old idiot."

Simon leaned back in his chair and said, "I can't seem to concentrate. Something's on my mind."

Simon is dark, good-looking, brilliant, and supremely self-confident. I didn't know anything ever bothered him. I couldn't wait to hear what he was going to say, and since no one looked meaningfully in my direction, I didn't feel like I had to disappear tactfully. It's just as well, because as I look back I realize that's how it all started.

"A mutt has been hanging around our house all week," he began.

"Have you been feeding it?" I asked.

Simon looked at me reproachfully. "Of course," he said. "It's starving." He went on, "The thing is, you'll hardly believe this . . . but there isn't any Humane Society in this town."

Simon might find it hard to believe because he's only lived here about a year, but I knew it perfectly well and had thought about it a hundred times.

"Sure there is," said Jack. "There has to be somebody who rounds up stray dogs. Animal Control, I think that's what they call it."

"That's just the cops," I said. "Sergeant Mulhoney comes and throws a net over them and they shoot them in the backyard of the police station."

"You're making that up!" Jack said.

"I am not. That's why Sergeant Mulhoney has put in for a transfer to the highway patrol. He hates it. I can't believe you didn't know that."

The thing about Jack, and all my family for that matter, is that he is so busy getting things done that he doesn't always see what is going on around him.

"What am I supposed to do?" asked Simon. "I can't turn this pathetic mutt who trusts me over to the police. But he's got the worst case of mange I've ever seen. What if Trixie catches it?"

Simon was devoted to Trixie, the handkerchief-sized Pomeranian who ruled over the little fenced yard at Simon's house. One of the few human things I had noticed about Simon was the way he cooed over Trixie. I thought it was sweet. It showed he wasn't all hung up on a macho image, if you know what I mean. But let's face it, if you have Simon's self-confidence, you don't need to own an attack dog to assert yourself.

"Mange on a Pomeranian is no joke," said Simon glumly.

"You should catch this stray dog yourself and take it to the vet," I said.

"If he's as bad off as Simon thinks," said Jack, "he may be past curing."

"Well, sitting around prophesying doom won't get you anywhere," I pointed out. "Is Simon going to do something about the dog or isn't he?"

I had noticed before that there is something about other people's problems that inspires me to come to crisp, intelligent decisions. It's only my own problems that paralyze me. I even volunteered to take the stray to the vet myself since Simon, like Jack, had a summer job.

So the next morning found me in front of Simon's house, a doggie burger in my hands, calling in a wheedling voice, "Here, doggie. Here, nice doggie." Trixie, in the fenced yard, sensed something was up, or perhaps she just smelled the dog food, but she yipped wildly and threw herself against the fence with all the force of her three pounds. Shortly, an enormous black mutt slowly inched his way out of the wooded lot next to Simon's house. His head was low and he was smiling a broad, humble smile, poor thing. He came right up to me and snatched the doggie burger out of my hands. While he gobbled it up, I quickly slipped a choke collar on him. He was obviously a gentle, friendly dog. That was what Simon had said, and luckily he was right because my catching a strange dog like that showed more courage than good sense. He was as big as the hound of the Baskervilles and was in perfectly terrible shape. I'll spare you the grisly details, but it was clear this dog needed a vet. I led him to the car and snapped the leash over the door handle in the back seat. He lay down meekly on the car seat and whimpered while I drove to the vet.

The long and the short of it was that Dr. Briggs kindly explained to me that the dog was really too far gone to be treated. He needed to be put to sleep. "He won't feel a thing," he promised me. He could tell I felt terrible. How could he not? I cried all over Simon's money as I was paying him. I felt like a murderer. That poor dog had trusted me, and what had I done to him? "Put him out of his misery," said my sensible voice. "Saved him from a painful, lingering death," said my sensible voice. "Preserved him from being shot by Sergeant Mulhoney," the sensible part of me went on. But the sensible part of me must be only something like one percent. The rest of me was crying all over the steering wheel as I drove home.

When I walked into the house, I saw that Mom had already been home for lunch. There was a big note on the refrigerator door, "Brenna—Please pick up some milk for tonight. Letter from Aunt Betty is on dining room table. Love, Mom."

I saw that next to the letter on the table was a stack of summer reading Mom had fetched from the library for me. Cunningly sandwiched between some innocent fiction was the thin book *So You Want to Be a Stewardess?*

I emptied a tray of ice cubes into an ice bag and lay down, pressing the cold compress to my eyes. I decided to lie there until such time as I felt strong enough to face Aunt Betty's letter—say Christmas. What had happened to the fun, fun summer I had dreamed of all through the school year? I thought of Dee Dee Mullins' family who always say to her—I've heard them say it—"Be sure and have a good time, honey." Why wasn't I born into a family like that? And why had I volunteered to solve Simon's problem for him? He should be the one lying here with the cold compress. I lay there for some time thinking these bitter thoughts.

Finally, I realized that no matter how awful I felt, I was going to have to go out and pick up the milk. So I dragged myself up and went to the A&P. The parking lot of the store was not thronged. The rush these days comes on the weekends and after five when people stop by on their way home from work to pick up things. I don't know if you've noticed this, but these days almost everybody has a job. Even Dee Dee

Mullins, whose mother just wants her to have a good time, had got a summer job. So this hot afternoon as I drove up, the only ones you could see in the parking lot were an elderly lady who was standing with her cane while a cab driver lifted her groceries into the back seat of the taxi, and a large sheep dog.

When I came out with the milk, the elderly lady and her cab were gone, but the sheep dog was still there, sitting by my car. Next to him, the car looked small.

"What are you doing here, fella?" I asked. "Are you lost?" His coat was full of sand spurs, but I didn't take this for a sign of long neglect. A long-haired dog can get in that shape in a single romp through a field. "Let me see your collar, fella," I said. He stood smiling at me while I felt through his hair for a collar. There didn't seem to be one. I wondered if he had slipped out of it. "Where do you live, boy?" I asked. But he just smiled at me. He was certainly cheerful. "Go home," I said. "Go home." He didn't budge. I opened the car door to hoist the milk in. In jumped the sheep dog. He sat on the front seat looking at the windshield, then gazed at me in a calm, friendly fashion as if to say, "When are we leaving?"

As a matter of fact, I'm not sure I could have gotten him out of the front seat if I had tried. He was a big dog and he clearly wanted to ride. But I didn't try. After my horrible experience at the vet, I wasn't in any shape to take a firm line. So I drove home. The sheep dog sat next to me, peering out the window like an unusually shaggy person taking an intelligent interest in the scenery. When we paused at the stoplight on Gay Street I saw that the driver in the next car did a double take. Probably at first glance it had looked like I was taking my grandfather to the dentist or something. There was an undoglike dignity about the sheep dog. It's hard to describe, but he was a very self-possessed animal. Actually, he reminded me a lot of Simon.

At the time all I thought was that this was sort of an unusual dog. It never occurred to me that afternoon that I was sharing the car with the cofounder of the Dog Protection Society, which is more or less the way it turned out to be.

2

The next morning I called the newspaper and put an ad in the "Found" column. I also called Sergeant Mulhoney at the police station in case someone had reported the dog missing there. I then set to work on the guest dog's coat. When Mom looked in on me at lunch, I was still at it and was so covered with white dog hairs I was beginning to look like a sheep dog myself. It was a big job.

"I'm surprised nobody has invented an automatic dog groomer," I said to Mom some minutes later as I bit into my sandwich. "Boy, there were a lot more sand spurs in there than I thought."

"You did put an ad in the newspaper, didn't you?"

"Uh-huh. I expect it won't be long before someone claims him."

"I hope you're right," said Mom. "Can you help me get that Victorian chest out of the garage? I finally sold that three corner cupboard and now I have room for it."

I am convinced that when my end comes it will be because I was flattened underneath a tottering Elizabethan sideboard. Mom seems to think that she and I and a dolly can move anything. But I didn't protest because I always had the faint hope that one day we would move enough of Mom's junk out of the garage that we would be able to put a car in there. This was probably sheer delusion on my part, but I never gave up hope. After we loaded the chest into the car trunk and Mom drove off, I returned to brushing Guest Dog. At times it didn't seem likely I would ever finish, but I did. Eventually I even managed to get the dog hair and revolting Victorian dust off my clothes.

Later that afternoon, I decided to take Guest Dog for a long walk into town to show off his beautifully groomed coat. I improvised a leash out of an old clothesline and set off. One of the things I like about our house is that it isn't very far from the center of town. Where we live is not like living way out in a modern subdivision. We live in one of the neighborhoods of dignified, older houses that were built close in and are actually part of the town, so it's not a very long walk to the town square. Even though it was a rather hot day for walking, I figured it would be a pleasant promenade.

It turned out to be fun to walk with Guest Dog. He was a dog with a sound sense of theater and he walked as if he were leading a parade. I felt as if just being with him made me look more dashing. I always thought I could use a little dash. I mean, when I look at my slightly light brown hair, my slightly greenish eyes, and the fairly good-looking but slightly ordinary rest of me, I sometimes wonder what a diamond necklace and a borzoi would do for me. Guest Dog wasn't exactly a borzoi—too dumpy for that—but he was the same sort of thing, quite an unusual-looking dog and definitely one with a lot of pizzazz. All brushed and clean, I thought we both looked very spiffy, especially if you didn't notice the clothesline.

We had a bit of excitement at the corner of Fourth and Broad when Guest Dog caught sight of a cat, but otherwise we had a nice, uneventful walk to the town square.

Oakdale has one of those standard town squares with a block of grass, six green benches, a Confederate monument, and a city hall. Today a man with a roaring lawnmower was cutting the grass, and as Guest Dog and I crossed the square we moved through the mixed smells of cut grass and exhaust fumes. I made my way to my favorite spot uptown, Mary's Donut Shop, which is just across the street from City Hall. At the donut shop they have a couple of tables outside with big blue umbrellas for shade, a perfect place for a person accompanied by a dog. I anchored Guest Dog to one of the white cast iron tables and got him a tall water and a handful of donut holes. He quickly slurped up the water, devoured the donut holes in a gulp, and began nibbling delicately on the paper cup. For myself, I had gotten a blueberry donut and a large milk. Putting them down on a spread out paper napkin, I settled down to think.

It's funny how blueberry donuts bring out the philosopher in me. "What is the meaning of life?" I asked myself, licking a little powdered sugar off. And more subtly, "What is the meaning of *my* life?" No immediate answer to this question presented itself, so I stretched my legs out in the sun in the hopes they would tan a little. It was warm and pleasant to sit watching traffic and sniffing exhaust fumes while before me the world went by—Volkswagens, stationwagons, the Sears delivery van. Suddenly the Sears delivery van swerved into the donut shop parking spaces right next to me and Simon climbed out. I may have mentioned that Simon has the sort of manner that makes you want to rock back on your heels and say, "Yes, my lord Count." Not very winning in his ways. But when he sat down next to me, with the glaring sunlight on him, I noticed little human touches about him for the first time, like the sun shining on the light hairs on his arm. I saw his dark eyebrows were high curved, like question marks. Guest Dog licked his extended hand and grinned at him inanely. Simon said, "I'm really sorry about the dog, Bren. Jack told me."

At this point the blueberry donut failed to sustain me. Tears welled up in my eyes. "It was for the best," I hiccuped pitifully.

Simon looked worried, as well he might. I daresay few people can face a crying, hiccuping girl with equanimity. "Look, I've got to go deliver this television set," he said. "I just had to stop and apologize for laying that on you." He ruffled Guest Dog's fur. "Who's your new friend?"

"I'm only keeping him *hiccup* until his owners claim him. I put *hiccup* an ad in the paper."

Simon gave me a comforting pat on the shoulder, then swung his door open and hopped up into the van. "Try holding your breath," he called as he drove off. I watched the Sears van pause at the light on the corner and then turn down Greenacre Street. I held my breath and hiccuped. Then I wiped my eyes and went back for another blueberry donut. I certainly needed something to cheer me up.

It suddenly hit me that what I wanted out of life was to be a heroine. You know what a heroine is. She's the girl who wins the game, snares the boy, and has the snappy comeback. Equally important —she does *not* hiccup.

On the way home Guest Dog tried to take a short cut through an inviting field full of sand spurs and beggar weed, but I firmly reined him in. I hadn't spent the whole morning with brush and

comb so he could undo it all tiptoeing through
beggar weed.

All the way home, I kept brooding about my
hiccupping in front of Simon. It did seem unfair.
Here he had stopped especially to say something
personal to me and I had to go and hiccup. No
doubt in the future he would limit his remarks to
me to the sort of thing I usually rate as Jack's
sister, like, "Hi. Is Jack home?" That had never
bothered me before, but suddenly today I felt low
about it. I guess what was going on was that now I
could see that when Simon turned the full light of
his personality on you even for a minute, he sort
of warmed you all over. It was funny I had never
noticed it before. When he talked to you as one
person to another, you just didn't think about
how arrogant he sometimes looked.

That evening Jack wasn't home for dinner. He
had checked in only briefly for a shower and some
energetic gargling with mouthwash before rushing
off to his dinner date. This created a perfect setup
for Mom and Dad to pounce on me about my
personal flaws since while Jack was gone I was
outnumbered. But actually they showed great
restraint, all things considered.

"Did you have a nice day, dear?" said Mom, as
she ladled out the spaghetti.

"Uh-huh," I said.

"Why don't you tell us about it?"

I was not keen to go into it. After all, when I
said I brushed the dog, took a walk, and started
the water boiling for the spaghetti, it wasn't going

to sound as if I had much of a sense of direction, or indeed much of a life.

"Why don't you tell me about your day first," I said cannily. This ploy turned out to be wildly successful as Mom's and Dad's days had been so interesting that they hadn't finished talking about them when I brought the ice cream out. Mom had had an exciting find while spending her coffee break strolling incognito through a rival shop to sneer at their inferior merchandise. Unexpectedly she had spotted a small but exquisite tea set of Limoges china, very underpriced and, her heart pounding, had bought it from the shop assistant. "Charlie doesn't know anything about china," she said happily. "I'll bet it's the first time he's ever even had a piece of china in the shop. He should stick to his own field."

Dad's mind was running on a different channel —the inadequacies of one of his partners. "That's terrific, Ellie," he said absently. "Did I tell you about Treviathan's latest? Today Mrs. Manson came in to get her will and Treviathan hadn't even started on it—if you can believe that—hadn't even started on it and it's been two weeks. He just smiled in that oily way of his and said it was almost ready. It's embarrassing to be associated with him, that's all," said Dad, swatting his napkin on the table forcefully. "I read an article the other day," he said, "about how more and more people are giving up their careers and turning to lives of religion and contemplation."

His voice took on a wistful note, "If only I could believe that Treviathan would do that."

I was glad to see the last bite of chocolate ice cream disappear before I could be called upon to tell how I had spent my day brushing Guest Dog. I jumped up with alacrity to clear the table.

"We never got to hear about Brenna's day, George," I heard Mother say with surprise. I turned on the garbage disposal and hummed a little tune.

Shortly after dinner Simon appeared at the door. "Hi!" he said. "Is Jack home?"

Just as I thought. Back to my role as Jack's sister. It seemed to me I had a hard and bitter life.

"He went out to dinner," I said. "I expect he won't be in until fairly late."

"I just wanted to give this back to him," said Simon, holding out Jack's copy of *Fifty Nifty Chess Openings*. I accepted temporary custody of it. Now that I was back to being just Jack's sister there seemed nothing to say. With a lordly wave he turned to go.

"Simon," I called, as he was getting into his car. "How often would you say you brush Trixie?"

"Every night," he said. "It's better if you don't let yourself get behind with it."

Then he sped away into the night.

Here was food for thought. Brushing every night was one thing on Trixie, where you were dealing in millimeters, and entirely something else on Guest Dog, where you were dealing in acres. I began to hope Guest Dog would be claimed by his owners very soon.

The rest of the evening I waited for a phone call from Guest Dog's owners, but the only calls we got were from a client of Dad who seemed to be indignant to learn he couldn't set fire to his own business to collect a tax loss, and a girl who wanted to talk to Jack. I found my mind absently turning to Simon. I wondered what he was like as a person. What did I know about him, really, even though he and Jack were friends? For one thing, it seemed odd, when I thought about it, that Simon should drive such a snazzy car while he and his mother lived in that tiny little house. I didn't like to ask Jack anything. Jack is so devoid of curiosity about people that I knew he would find my interest in Simon's affairs very peculiar.

The next morning, following Simon's advice, I had again brushed Guest Dog, who judging from the state of his coat appeared to have spent a restless night. He loved the attention and stood there, his vast red tongue lolling out in apparent perfect happiness. The brushing was nothing like as difficult as it had been yesterday, but as I very slowly progressed inch by inch from nose to tail, it did cross my mind to wonder whether instead of searching for him anxiously, Guest Dog's rightful owners had uttered a whoop of joy on discovering him gone and had replaced him with a Chihua-hua.

Midmorning the phone rang, but it was just

Sergeant Mulhoney. "Anyone ever claimed that sheep dog, Brenna?" he asked.

"Not yet," I said. "But I'm hoping somebody might see the ad on Thursday." That's when garage sales are advertised in our town and it's when most people read the classified ads.

"So you're just going to take care of him until these people show?" he asked.

"I guess so," I said.

"The thing is," he said, "we've got a dog in here that nobody has claimed for ten days, and . . . well, it's supposed to be curtains for him today."

My charitable impulses, I noticed, had been somewhat dulled by my experience with Guest Dog. "What kind of coat does this dog have?" I inquired.

"What do you mean?" he said. "It's just an ordinary dog."

"I mean does it have long hair?"

"No, no. I figure it's part dachshund and part something else."

"I guess I could keep it a few days," I said dubiously, "since it's an emergency." I wasn't too sure how my parents would view the new boarder.

"You could? Oh, great! Terrific! I really appreciate this, Brenna," he said warmly.

Sergeant Mulhoney arrived bearing the problem dog with a speed that bore testimony to the lack of pressing criminal cases around here. His gratitude was touching, and really the dog was adorable. I could see why poor Sergeant Mulhoney was fond of the little critter. He had a cute little terrier-type smile, perky ears, and a definitely long, low profile. You wouldn't say he was a great classical beauty, of course, but there was a certain clownish charm. I surveyed him thoughtfully. You would certainly imagine, I thought, that a home could be found for a dog like this. You really would.

Luckily Guest Dog treated the funny-looking newcomer with condescension instead of outright hostility. And the new little dog was so well-behaved and cheerful that it was actually two days before my parents even realized he was there. I didn't feel like I had to bring up the matter earlier because after all he was just staying with me temporarily. I made this perfectly plain to Mom when she tripped over the dog making her way out of the toolshed carrying a nineteenth-century bread safe. I don't have to tell you that our toolshed is filled not with tools but with old furniture. "*Eeeeek!*" she shrieked. "What is that dog doing in here, Brenna? I nearly killed myself tripping over him." She gripped the bread safe tightly.

I regarded the dog with fond pride. "Kind of cute, isn't he? I'm just keeping him for Sergeant Mulhoney temporarily. They were going to shoot him, poor little thing."

Mom, who is not a bad sort, softened at once. "But sweetheart, you can't just take in every stray in town. You just can't."

"Oh, I know! I told Sergeant Mulhoney this would have to be just an emergency measure. I made that perfectly plain."

If it was perfectly plain to me, it was clearly not as plain to Sergeant Mulhoney, who had not appeared to collect the dog by the end of the week. Furthermore, Thursday's classified ads appeared without Guest Dog's owners rushing to his side.

All that was bad enough, but that same day I was dismayed to find little Tommy Meadows standing at the front door. He was holding a puppy. "My mom won't let me keep it," he said, coming to the point at once.

"Where did you get it from?" I asked.

"Boy at school."

"Well, why don't you take it back to the boy at school and explain that your mother won't let you keep it." I smiled, pleased with myself and my fine reasoning.

"Tried that," said Tommy. "He won't take it."

Of course, he won't take it, I thought, casting curses on the head of the absent schoolboy who was visiting this problem on me. Nobody but me would be so soft-headed as to take it. I opened my mouth to try to make Tommy see reason, but gave up. Why waste my breath? It was written in the stars that I was going to end up taking care of this puppy. I knew it before I said the first word. What was the point in struggling against destiny? Resignedly, I let Tommy hand it to me.

"I'll try to find a home for him," I said with a

sigh, "but next time, Tommy, remember that a puppy is a big responsibility."

"Yes, ma'am."

"And check with your mother before you take another one."

"Yes, ma'am."

I sighed again and closed the door. Tommy made his way back home, light-hearted and carefree. I made my way to the backyard carrying an additional problem. I could see that I was going to have to take steps. I might not have to tell Mom and Dad about the new addition to the household right away, but I knew that when I did tell them, I had better have a plan for these dogs' future.

3

FREE DOG TO GOOD HOME," I typed on index cards. I did twenty-five of these and another twenty-five of "FREE PUPPY TO GOOD HOME," each with my phone number on them. I surveyed my stack of index cards with satisfaction. I had tried the classified ad approach to the guest-dog problem with no result and at a cost of $7.50. It was time to try a grass roots approach. In our town, as in most places, you can often find community bulletin boards where people put little cards advertising apartments for rent, piano lessons, used Hondas, and whatnot. The beauty of these bulletin boards is that you can use them free. The problem with them is that they are scattered here and there all over town, and I wasn't exactly sure where.

And I had another problem. More often than not, Mom leaves her car at home for me and walks back and forth from the shop, but today she had taken the car to an estate sale in nearby Castalia. In order to get any place today I had no choice but to pull out my old bicycle. I threw a pack of thumbtacks and the index cards in the basket and rode off down the driveway, scattering gravel as I went. It was essential that I get moving on this immediately. I wanted to be able to report progress at the supper table tonight before Mom and Dad noticed the puppy gamboling around the back yard with the two other dogs.

I knew I had seen one of these bulletin boards at the laundromat in a neighborhood shopping center only a few blocks from us, so I headed towards there. When I arrived the laundromat turned out to be full of women with lint on their jeans and toddlers trailing after them. It was hard to believe they would be yearning for the additional responsibility of a dog, but I put my first advertisement up there. I found another bulletin board at a drug store at the other end of the shopping center. The board wasn't in too prominent a location—in a corner by a water fountain—but at least, I reasoned, during the summer a lot of people were drinking water. I drank a good deal of water myself. It was getting hot. Then I

skewered my notice on the board with a thumb-
tack.

The next shopping area was a mile and a half
away, and I was beginning to pant, but I began
pedaling resolutely in that direction. The houses
which had whizzed by when I had set off merrily
this morning now seemed to have slowed considerably and my legs were beginning to feel heavier.
It was amazing how hot it had gotten.

By the time I arrived at West Garden Shopping
Plaza, the glaring midday sun was beating down
on the sidewalks and I had definitely wilted. I
limped to the laundromat. No bulletin board. I
tried the drugstore. No bulletin board. I searched
the place from hardware store to pizza parlor
without finding a place to put my ad. I realized
now I should have done a little preliminary research by phone to find out exactly who had these
things and who didn't, but it was too late now.

I decided I had better try at least one more
shopping area before I turned homeward, so I
painfully got on my bike again. I decided all this
exercise was going to be great for my figure, if I
didn't pass out from sun stroke.

The distance from West Garden Shopping
Plaza to Walnut Shopping Plaza is a bit of a blur,
but I don't think I ran down any pedestrians.
Happily, the Walnut laundromat revealed a bulletin board. I sat down there for a minute to catch
my breath. Laundromats were clearly a good bet
in one respect. All these people washing clothes
had nothing to do but watch their clothes go

round and round. They had lots of time to read bulletin boards. A nearby woman in curlers opened her dryer, and I was hit by a fresh blast of hot air. I pulled myself to my feet and staggered out to the sidewalk.

It was noon by now, and besides being exhausted, I was starving. It occurred to me that if I sat down in air conditioning and ate lunch, I might be able to summon the strength afterwards to take in one or two more shopping areas. I pushed my bike down the walk to the drugstore. Then I locked it and parked it right by the door where I could see it, as I don't trust human nature too far when it comes to bicycles. I plunged into the drugstore air conditioning and made my way, past the indigestion remedies, to the lunch counter. My heart gave a happy leap as I perceived that this drugstore had a bulletin board. Then it fell with a sickening thud when I realized that Simon was sitting at the lunch counter eating a hot dog. He was wearing a blue knit shirt, had a tall Coke at his elbow, and had the ineffable cool, superior look of someone who has been transported by the internal combustion engine rather than the humble bicycle. But there was no help for it. If I wanted anything to eat or drink I was going to have to say hello to him, even though I could feel the sweat dripping down my face.

"Hi, Simon," I said, falling exhaustedly onto a lunch counter stool. He smiled as if he were pleased to see me. Either that or I looked pretty funny, which I had to admit was also possible. I brushed a damp strand of hair out of my face.

"What are you doing way out here?" he asked. "You look like you've run the whole way."

I explained about my bulletin board approach and the new puppy which had made it all necessary.

"You're never going to be able to bicycle all over the whole town today," he said.

"I don't know why not," I said stoutly.

"It's just too far, kiddo. You'll pass out first." The waitress handed me my hot dog and I began eating it without comment, mostly because I thought Simon was probably right.

"Tell you what," he said kindly. "Wrap up your hot dog, hop in the delivery van, and I'll give you a ride to the other side of town. I have to deliver a sofa out there. You'll have to stay in the back of the van, though. I'm not supposed to carry hitchhikers."

"But what about my bike?" I protested.

"It'll go in the van."

So it was that I sat in the back of the delivery van with a new sofa, my bicycle, and the rest of my hot dog. It was hot. It was bumpy. It was crowded. But compared to bicycling another five miles, it had a lot to be said for it.

We went first to Nottingham Court, where Simon loaded the sofa onto a dolly and took it down the ramp and into the house. It was kind of pleasant to watch someone else hefting furniture about for a change. Then we stopped off at the Nottingham Road convenience store and put a notice on their bulletin board. The next stop was Briarwood Lane, where Simon had to deliver a stove. After that was the Sunnyside Shopping Plaza bulletin board, and we also left a notice on the bulletin board above the coupon trade center at the A&P. Altogether we got up three more notices.

Finally Simon decanted me at my own front door and helped me pull my bicycle out of the back of the van. My shirt was sticking moistly to my back. Even my fingers felt sticky. I asked myself what a heroine would do in these circumstances. I decided she would smile bravely, so I took a stab at it.

Simon regarded me sympathetically. "You'll feel better after a cold shower," he said. He got back in the truck. "Let me know how the ads work," he said. Then he drove off, one arm resting on the open window. The wind ruffled his hair a bit as he passed me with a wave. I noted bitterly that he looked cool.

I went in and took a cold shower, but I did not feel better. Not a bit. I don't expect much. I mean, I'm not the sort of girl who can't live with herself unless a guy is made breathless by her beauty. Nor is my week ruined if some guy fails to tell me he can't live without the light of my beautiful eyes. But I did feel I could stand getting a better response from Simon than "Hold your breath," or "Take a cold shower."

I changed my guinea pig's cage.

After that, determined to cheer myself up, I dug out the old red ball I've had since I was a baby and went out back to play with the three dogs. Guest Dog turned out to be more of a spectator than an athlete. He lay down by the hollyhocks and watched, his head turning amiably first left, then right, like a fan at Wimbledon. The puppy kept running all over very busily, her ears flapping and her fat little tummy barely clearing the ground, but she never managed to catch the ball. I'm not sure she even realized that was the point of the game. Clown Dog, however, turned out to be quite good at it. He snapped the ball in mid-air, blocked it as it rolled towards the hollyhocks and played shortstop to my attempts to throw it to the puppy. Clearly, this was a dog who would rather retrieve than eat. All the while Guest Dog watched peacefully. When Clown Dog finally threw himself down on the grass panting, Guest Dog slowly got up, walked over, and nuzzled him, no doubt offering him congratulations on his fielding technique and then sat down in front of me hopefully, as if he expected the encore might be bones all around.

The encore I had in mind, however, was not so pleasant as that. During all the running about, I had noticed a distressing tendency on the part of the participants to pause for a good scratch. I had decided I couldn't put off any longer dipping the dogs for fleas. I had already bought the dip, but I wasn't looking forward to using it.

I fetched it down from the top shelf of the toolshed and read the directions carefully. That caused me to be so paralyzed with fear I could hardly proceed from there. But I went in the house and gathered up boots, a shower cap, rubber gloves, old clothes, and goggles. Once I had fully garbed myself from head to toe like a space traveller, I filled a washtub with the foul smelling dip. Then all I had to do was get hold of the dogs. Puppy was, I felt, too little to dip, and Clown Dog proved to be easy—in and out in no time, a smile for everyone. But Guest Dog was obviously going to be a challenge. He had obviously had some experience with dip. At the first whiff of it he retired to the far end of the yard. He didn't actually so lose his dignity that he ran from me, but as soon as I got almost close enough to grab him he would get up and quietly move away as if he just happened to want to smell a buttercup in a distant patch of grass.

Finally I had an inspiration. "Come here, puppy. Here, puppy," I called. I put the puppy in my lap and began to tousle it. "Good dog! What a fine puppy! What a wonderful puppy!" I cooed.

Guest Dog began to look a little uneasy. You could see the germ of an unpleasant idea beginning to develop in his mind. He was getting overlooked, perhaps even supplanted by a perfidious young pup. Shortly he began to amble casually towards me. At first not very close, but then close enough. Suddenly I grabbed at him. Puppy was thrown sprawling as Guest Dog took off, but

I held on tight. That sheep dog turned out to be as much muscle as fluff; he dragged me fifteen feet before I managed to put on the brakes by digging my heels into the turf. I dragged him to the washtub, his head hanging.

Success at last. But I knew he would never fall for this trick twice. Next time I would have to take care to tie him up before the dip made its appearance.

I picked him up and dumped him unceremoniously into the washtub. His enormous coat at once sopped up all the dip leaving the tub empty. Then he jumped out of the tub and shook himself all over, hard, flinging gallons of dip in all directions with hurricanelike force. In spite of my shower cap, boots, old clothes and goggles, I got a thorough dipping myself. I definitely needed another shower.

I made my way back to the house thinking that the way my luck was running Simon would probably show up any minute with *Chuckie's Favorite Checkmate Strategies* or something and see me in this state. But as it happened the only person who showed up was Mom.

"Goodness, Brenna, you look like a frog in those goggles," she said. "What a turn you gave me."

Guest Dog was rolling around in the grass trying to erase the smell of the dip. Who could blame him? I headed toward the shower.

When I got out, Mom was in the kitchen prying apart frozen pork chops. Her brow was creased.

"I see another dog has been added to the menagerie in back. What's going on?"

"Strictly temporary, Mom," I said, towelling my hair vigorously. I told her about my day's effort putting signs on all the bulletin boards in town.

"That may not be enough," she said. "I'll treat you to another week's worth of ads in the paper."

I appreciated that because even $7.50 made inroads into my store of babysitting money. Babysitting slacks off a good deal in the summer when people go on vacation, and I began to regret that I had frivolously squandered my spring babysitting gains on dresses instead of saving for dog food. Guest Dog really packed it away.

"And Brenna," Mom said seriously, *"no more dogs."*

"Right," I agreed. "No more dogs." I stood away from the breakfast bar to brush my hair out.

"Have you given any more thought to Betty's offer, dear?" Mom asked.

"Well, I need to get the dogs taken care of first," I hedged. I thought it wise to change the subject. "What do you know about Simon, Mom?" I said.

"Jack's friend? He seems to be a very hardworking conscientious boy." She took a taste of the potato salad and added more salt.

"He's unusual, don't you think?"

"I don't think I know what you mean, dear."

Sometimes it seemed to me that my family was more than a little oblivious. I wrapped the towel around my hair, pulled up a chair, and began to slice celery for the salad. No matter what mother said, I thought, it was obvious that Simon was an unusual type. That let-'em-eat-cake attitude might have been common once among the crowned heads of Europe, but it set him apart in modern Oakdale. I thought about the other things that set him apart—his black eyebrows and the way his hair curled under the slightest bit at the nape of his neck. Then I noticed I was slicing the celery slower and slower and got a grip on myself. Maybe Mom and Dad were right, I thought, about my needing direction to my life. Certainly nothing showed a deterioration of my mind so much as sitting here thinking about the hair curling on Simon's neck.

I decided to think about Gary Potter instead, a person who was superior to Simon in at least one notable respect—he had asked me out. When Gary had told me his family was going on vacation, I had not marked the dates on my calendar in red, but surely they should be getting back by now. Possibly he would call me up and ask me to a movie or a picnic. A movie would be better really because you didn't have to talk and Gary wasn't exactly a raconteur.

"You only need to slice the celery, Brenna," said Mom, "not puree it." I came to my senses and saw that the cutting board was covered with teensy little moist bits of celery. I swept them into the salad bowl with simple dignity.

On Wednesday, the fourth dog arrived. I had

just been vacuuming the living room, where the dust was getting out of hand. When I switched off the vacuum I heard a scratching sound. It seemed to be coming from the front door. It wasn't like the scratching sound a branch makes rubbing against the house; it was more insistent than that. I coiled up the cord to the vacuum cleaner and went to investigate. When I opened the front door, a beagle met my gaze. It had been tied to the banister of the front porch and now evidently wanted in. Obviously it was a foundling. I had become known overnight as someone on whom to dump unwanted animals. My heart sank.

To think I had imagined the situation was desperate when I had inherited the puppy from Tommy. That wasn't desperate—*this* was. Mom had said no more dogs and she unquestionably meant it.

For the first time in my life, I blessed my lucky stars that Mom and Dad, the workaholics, could be trusted not to pull themselves away from their work until after six. I needed time.

My mind was racing wildly. I remembered how beagles don't bark but instead bay in a tone reminiscent of graveyards at midnight. I saw how the critter's paws turned out, ducklike, the sign of an efficient digger. I recalled how Mary Sue's beagle had been expelled from obedience school for insubordination. The beagle, unmindful of my thoughts, wagged its tail at me cheerily.

It was clear I couldn't keep this dog. Even apart

from what Mom and Dad thought, I had as much dog as I could handle. Our backyard was beginning to look distinctly overpopulated and Mom had dropped the subject of my visiting Aunt Betty. It was all too clear I had to hang around to dip, brush, feed, and exercise the animals.

Who can I get to take care of this dog? I thought desperately. And then the answer came to me. Someone who already owned a beagle. Someone with established, certified beagle tolerance, preferably someone living far, far out in the country.

Leaving the beagle tied to the railing, I dashed inside to consult my school yearbook. I scanned the faces quickly. At this point, Jack and Simon walked in together. "Hey, Bren," said Jack, opening the refrigerator, "what's with the beagle? I thought you had your dog quota." He poured out a couple of glasses of milk and began stacking cheese, bread, bologna, and peanut butter on a tray. Jack routinely needed these sorts of provisions to sustain life until dinner. "And what have you got your yearbook out for, for Pete's sake," he said. His carefree tone set my teeth on edge.

"I am looking for a kind, beagly face," I said calmly.

Jack chortled.

"I mean I am looking for someone who could take care of this dog until we can find it a permanent home," I said carefully, showing my strength of character in refusing to give way to the impulse to strangle him. "I feel I need someone who already has a beagle and knows their little ways."

"What about Mary Sue?"

"Don't you remember? Her parents found a good home for theirs on a Texas ranch and bought her a parakeet instead."

"What about Jeff Feldon," said Simon. "I think he has a beagle."

"But I don't know Jeff Feldon," I said.

"I do though." Simon took the phone from me and called Jeff but got no answer. "This isn't the best time of year," he said. "People are going on vacation. Who do you know who has a beagle, Jack?"

"Good grief, I don't know."

"What we need is a list," I said. "That way if we call someone and get no answer, we can make a note of it to call back, and that way we can be sure we don't call the same person twice."

"The woman is a genius for organization," said Simon warmly, pulling a pen out of his pocket.

This was the nicest thing Simon had ever said to me. My heart fluttered dangerously. However, I maintained an appearance of calm, took the pen from him, and began a list.

"Now who do we know who either has a beagle, has had a beagle, or might have a beagle? Also, who do we know who has already been on vacation?"

Simon and Jack haltingly came up with a few names. I added some more, and we had a fairly respectable little list. But when I sat down at the telephone and started trying to tie down someone definite, the list began to shrink alarmingly. Three weren't home, two were going on vacation any minute, and four were sure their mothers wouldn't let them take another dog. While I was gathering these discouraging responses, Simon and Jack worked on dinner. Jack had arranged for him and Simon to treat the family to homemade pizza tonight, and they were busy rolling out dough, simmering and tasting tomato sauce, and finding a cutting board on which to slice the mushrooms and pepperoni.

"I think we need to take a different tack," I said thoughtfully. "Except for our friends, we don't know who has a beagle and we don't know who is about to go on vacation. I think we should try some farm kids. I don't think farmers go in as much for vacations. Somebody has to mind the cows and all that."

"I don't know," said Jack dubiously. "I think they call the farms around here agribusinesses, and they don't raise cows." Still, he left the tomato sauce and came over to flip to the year-book's group shot of Future Farmers of America.

"I think," volunteered Simon, "that since we're going through all this, we ought to look to the long term. It looks like Brenna may keep getting dogs dumped on her and we should be ready."

I could see the logic of it. "You're right," I said. "Instead of asking these farm kids if they will keep a beagle, we should ask if they're willing to board a dog on a temporary basis. We'll ask if we can put them on our permanent list of boarders." I could see the whole thing before me now. We would have a chain of temporary homes for the dogs. As one was placed in a permanent home it would make room for another to board on a farm or with someone who had a big backyard.

"It's a community service, really," I said slowly. "You know, a charity. We should get a name and appeal for help with the food and expenses." I sat down and began chewing on the pen reflectively. "We'll call it the Dog Protection Society." I was beginning to think big.

After the pepperoni was sliced, Simon took a turn at the phone while I washed lettuce for the salad. He finally reached Tony Harris, who lives on a small tobacco farm five miles out of town, and got him to agree to take care of the beagle until we could find a permanent home for it.

"I think someone had better take that beagle to Tony right now," I said when he hung up. "I don't want Mom and Dad to find it tied to the banister when they get in."

"I'll take it," said Simon. "I know where Tony lives. It's going to make me a bit late to dinner though."

"Worth it," I said.

"I'll just hold off a bit putting the pizza in," Jack said. "I think Brenna's right. It's better to get the beagle out of sight right away. The way dogs are piling up in the backyard, you can't expect Mom and Dad are going to react rationally to the sight of another one."

"Tell Tony we'll provide the food," I said rashly as Simon headed out. I had had a vision. It's a good thing Jack knew how to make a salad because I went into a trancelike state and wasn't much good for cooking after that. There was a lot to be thought out. How would we get donations of food? Who would vet the dogs, and how would we pay him? How could we efficiently put up dogs for adoption if they were boarded here and there all over the place on outlying farms? I was still meditatively chewing on the pen and thinking when Mom breezed in.

"Mary Jenkins finally bought that settle," she said. "She's been coming in and measuring it and prodding it for so long I had decided that looking at it was just a hobby with her. When she came in today and took out her checkbook I nearly fainted." She peered critically at the pizza laid out on the counter. "Looks good, dear," she said. "You don't think it needs more mozzarella?"

A moment later Dad strode in and tossed his briefcase on the family room couch. "What a day!" he groaned. He glanced at the pizza. "Too much mozzarella there, Jack. Why don't you just lift some of it off and save it for later."

Ignoring them both, Jack firmly shoved the pizza into the oven.

"There's no such thing as too much mozzarella, George," explained mother kindly. "Brenna, aren't you even going to say hello to us?"

"Hello," I said, releasing the pen from my teeth. "I'm thinking."

"Where's Simon?" asked Dad. "I thought he was coming for dinner."

"He had to take a beagle out to Tony Harris," explained Jack.

Mom and Dad looked at me accusingly. They seemed to imagine that if a beagle was involved I must have something to do with it.

"Someone left a beagle tied up on the front porch," I admitted. "Of course, we couldn't keep another dog so we've got Tony Harris to agree to board it temporarily."

"Now, Brenna," said Dad, "don't you think this dog business is getting a bit out of hand? How on earth are you going to find a home for this beagle, and what is Tony Harris going to do if you don't?"

"No, I don't think it's getting out of hand," I said. "I'm getting it under control. I haven't ironed out all the details yet, but I've got a plan."

"I eagerly await your ironing out all the details," Dad said wryly.

"This must be Simon," said Mom as the dogs set up a howl. It was moments like this that pointed out that we really did have enough dogs. They made a fairly unbelievable noise, and after all, we didn't want the neighbors forming a lynch mob.

Simon opened the door and stepped in. Outside, the din slowly subsided. He gave the okay signal to Jack and me, then turned his attention to greeting our parents. Simon delivered the polite conventionalities like a courtier. It's amazing what a little assurance will do for "Good evening, Mrs. Matthews, Mr. Matthews." It was interesting, too, how with those high eyebrows he could manage to look both amused and perfectly open and honest at the same time. There was an interesting question: with beetle brows would Simon lose his charm?

In a matter of minutes we were all sitting down to hot pizza. I am very fond of pizza when it's judiciously adorned with mushrooms and pepperoni. Indeed, anything at all is delicious on pizza except the noxious anchovy. I helped myself to a large slice right away as I know from experience how quickly Jack and my father can demolish a pizza. Simon immediately served himself two slices, suggesting that he, too, was no slouch in the pizza eating department. Mother, slow off the mark, looked a little alarmed at the quick shrinkage of the pizza.

"There's another one in the oven," Jack reassured her between mouthfuls.

Mother smiled graciously. She did not like for guests to get the impression that it was necessary to scramble fast for food at our table, though this was often, in fact, the case. "I understand your mother has gone back to school, Simon," said Mother, trying to find a conversational topic more lofty than pizza. "How does she like it?"

"She loves it, but it keeps her pretty busy. She's hoping to take the CPA exam in the spring."

"I admire her for it," said Dad. "It's not easy going to school and working at the same time. Does accounting interest you? I believe there's a lot of opportunity there."

"I think that's why Mother chose it," said Simon. "No, I am going to go into the import-export business with my father." There was a pause and he added, "I'm his only son, you see."

I looked at him curiously. He acted as if the import-export business had laws of succession, like a monarchy.

"That's why Simon keeps at the Spanish so hard, Mom," said Jack.

"But Jack tells me you speak Spanish beautifully," said Mom.

"I speak decent Spanish for an American," admitted Simon. "My family lived in the Dominican Republic until I was six, so I spoke Spanish then. In fact, my parents kept me back from the first grade an extra year to bring my English up to par. That's why I'm older than the other kids in my grade. But now it's my English that's fine and my Spanish that doesn't measure up." Simon's brow was creased. "I really can't let up on it a bit. I do conversation twice a week with Margarita— she's an exchange student here—and then I study literature once a week with Professor Posada at the college."

"Sounds like everyone's busy at your house," said Dad amiably. "Is your father a native speaker of Spanish?"

"No," said Simon, "but the next thing to it. He

calls me up every weekend from New York to talk." He added glumly, "In Spanish only. He likes to see how I'm coming along."

"And is he pretty satisfied so far?" asked Mom.

I thought that was a pretty tactless question considering the expression on Simon's face. But he suddenly grinned. "I don't know. My problem is that when he calls I feel about six and probably sound that way, too."

During all this, I was certainly listening to what was being said, but I was looking more than listening. I was thinking that Simon looked like a Corsican bandit. I munched thoughtfully on my pizza. He wasn't just pleasantly washed out, like our family, but very vivid looking—black hair, blue eyes, entrancing temples. It was nice to have him at the table, I thought, whether he paid any attention to me or not. After all, you don't have to own Sequoia National Park to appreciate it. It's nice just knowing it's there.

I sat there chewing my pizza and thinking kind thoughts, my good will spilling in all directions. I looked at Mom—how elegantly she used a knife and fork. Dad—what kind eyes he had. And Jack—his appetite was really remarkable. Everyone at the table seemed at that moment to be really excellent people. I was just in that kind of good mood. What had happened was that I had hatched some interesting plans for the Dog Protection Society. I could see it all falling into place and could envision the glorious future of the society. The warm glow created by these happy ideas was simply spilling in all directions when I looked at the people around the table.

Of course, I had a long way to go in organizing the society. After dinner I helped Jack and Simon clean up. My hidden motive in helping was to seize the chance to enlist their help with my scheme.

I cleared my throat. "The Dog Protection Society," I said, stacking the silverware. They looked at me expectantly. "The Dog Protection Society," I intoned, "is a community service. We should try to get help paying for the dog food."

"I think you're right," said Jack. "I have a feeling this beagle won't be the last, Brenna. You're getting in this thing pretty deep."

This did not exactly strike the note of optimism I had hoped for, but at least he agreed with me.

"My idea," I said, "is to put bins in the supermarkets where people can put donated dog food. We need something eye catching." I warmed to my subject. "What I envision is a dog-shaped box with a big open mouth that the dog food can be dropped into. That will get our point across. That we need to feed the dogs, I mean. I think the donation of dog food will work better than asking for money because when you ask for money people always give nickles or quarters. If we ask for dog food, that will bring in bigger donations."

"If any donations come in at all," said Jack.

"I think there may be some technical problems with making a dog-shaped box," said Simon, who had started sketching a plan for the box on a scrap of paper.

"Besides," said Jack, "what if you can't get the owner's permission to put the boxes in the stores. It would be silly for us to make all those boxes and then find out we couldn't even use them."

I had to admit that Jack had a point there. I was going to have to do a little preliminary work to make sure we could find a place for the boxes. But I was anxious not to let my workers escape.

"Okay," I said. "Tomorrow I'll go out and try to get permission from some store managers. But if I'm able to do that, will you two help me make the boxes tomorrow night?"

To my relief they agreed.

I had a hard time getting to sleep that night. I couldn't seem to stop rehearsing what I might say to the store managers the next day. "Mr. Smith, you know this problem we have with stray dogs?" I would begin in my mind. No. Be direct. "I wonder if I could have your permission?" No. "Wonder" was not good. Why sound doubtful? Polite but confident should be the tone. I kept going over and over what I could say, trying to figure out something polite but confident.

Another thing that worried me was that they might not take me seriously because I was so young. Maybe they would think I didn't know what I was doing.

Then, as I watched the moonlight make patterns on the wall where it seeped in around the blinds, I suddenly had a bright idea. I would get

Sergeant Mulhoney to make the first contact for me. After all, he owed me a favor, and besides he should have a personal interest in getting the Dog Protection Society going. Yes. That's what I would do. Tomorrow I would speak to Sergeant Mulhoney. If he could just get one store to take the box, I felt that would be all I needed. It would be a starting point when I went to talk to the store managers. I could say, "Mr. Blank let us put a box in his store. Would you let us, too?" Maybe then there would be a kind of domino effect and everyone would be eager not to be left out. The part of my mind that was still awake recognized that this was drifting into a fantasy scenario, but then there wasn't much of my mind awake at that point. Feeling more peaceful now that my main problem was solved, I finally was able to fall asleep.

4

Sergeant Mulhoney blanched when I showed up at his desk the next morning. He obviously imagined I was returning Clown Dog to his care. It was just as well he thought that because it meant he was positively relieved when I asked him to make an appeal to a store manager for me.

"I don't think I'd better do it in uniform," he said. "It's not exactly like collecting for the Police Benevolent Fund."

I opened my mouth to speak and he hastily added, "But I'd be happy to do it, go on over to Piggly Wiggly after my shift ends, lay hold of

57

Marty Smith and put the bite on him. Heh, heh, put the bite on him. That's pretty good. Then I'll give you a call to let you know what he says." He stood up to open the door for me and composed his merry face into an expression of suitable gravity. "After all, it's a very worthwhile thing you're doing."

It certainly was. Once home, I commenced my usual doggy routine of brushing and feeding the dogs, then policing the backyard. The fleas seemed to be under control now, but I knew that it being summertime, I would have to be alert for them.

I began working on my first donation box. I wanted to be able to show store managers a sample box. Although I had originally planned something fancier, Simon was right and I ran into technical difficulties. I finally settled on a simple, large square box design. I covered the whole box with brown paper and sketched in legs to make it look like the body of a sitting dog. The entire front of the box was to be the dog's face. It was a sort of comic strip depiction of a dog, but you could certainly make out what it was.

My best idea was draping a piece of red cloth on the inside of the hole for the dog's mouth, the opening that the food was to be dropped into. When the rest of the dog's face was painted in, the red cloth covering the opening was his large red tongue. The food could be handily dumped into the opening, the red curtain flapping closed again

after each bag was deposited. A simple white sign
went on top of the box:

> FEED ME. DROP BAGS AND CANS OF
> DOG FOOD HERE TO HELP IN THE
> WORK OF THE DOG PROTECTION SO-
> CIETY.

I painted in sad brown eyes above the red curtain.
With an extra flourish I painted in a few brown
spots on the dog, then surveyed my work with
pleasure. This was a dog you wanted to help.

At first I was very nervous about approaching
the store managers for permission, but it didn't
turn out to be too difficult. At Safeway I began by
telling how we were putting a box in at Piggly
Wiggly. At the A&P I told them about the boxes I
was putting in at Safeway and Piggly Wiggly, and
so on. None of the managers were exactly excited
about having doggy boxes in their stores, but they
were resigned to helping in community appeals.
You only had to walk through the automatic
doors past signs advertising the YWCA Swim-
arama and the First Baptist Bake Sale to realize
that charity had trod this path before.

When I finished I had six permissions. Now all I
needed was six artistically crafted doggie boxes,
so when I left my last grocery store manager, I
turned the car's nose to the back of the shopping
center where cardboard boxes are commonly to
be found. It was beginning to look like rain and a

gust of wind was blowing a crumpled white paper bag along the alley. I got out of the car and picked my way past some broken crates. Then I stood on tiptoe and peered into the Dempster Dumpster shared by several shops, and a pizza parlor, a disillusioning sight.

I hadn't noticed it before, but when it comes to disposing of garbage, people can be very sloppy. Wet tea bags, half-eaten hamburgers, and cigarette ashes were spread all over otherwise perfectly fine doggie boxes. At the next Dempster Dumpster, behind K-Mart, I did manage to hook a decent box, but the Dumpster at the grocery store proved a complete disappointment. Here, far from being sloppy, the grocery store had gone overboard with neatness and had cut their hundreds of boxes up into equal cardboard squares bound into fat bundles with metal bands.

Getting back in the car, I headed a couple of blocks down to the parking lot of a liquor store. Liquor stores are known for their sturdy, high quality boxes, but this one must have just had its garbage picked up because I only got two boxes. Now fat drops of rain were falling. I threw the boxes in the back seat, jumped in the car, and rolled up the windows. The rain began to pour. I knew box hunting was a lost cause now. The rain would be turning boxes all over town into cardboard mush. With a sigh I headed home. I hoped that Jack would have the foresight to pick up some boxes wherever he was. As his summer job was digging cable trenches for the phone company, his work took him far afield. But wherever he was today, surely boxes could be found. After all, they have to put those cables in something, right?

Later, just before dinner, I was a little annoyed to see that Jack came in without so much as a box to his name. I did not say anything sharp, however. It was important not to alienate my workers.

"I was sort of hoping you would bring home some boxes," I said delicately. "I was only able to find three."

"I thought you would be getting them all," said Jack. "Anyway, I didn't have the time. We lost half an hour when it rained and I just now got off." He headed to the shower to remove the dirt and mud deposited on him by a day of ditch digging.

After dinner, Simon showed up to help with the project. Luckily, he came in the door dragging three boxes. I helped him pull them into the family room.

"These are perfect!" I said.

"Got them at the moving company on Hill Street," he said.

I could see that Simon had foresight and ingenuity. Not to mention beautiful eyes. Jack and I dug out rolls of brown wrapping paper from the hall closet for us to cover the boxes with. This was so our doggie faces would have a smooth and finished look, which they would not have if Big Boy's Baked Beans and other box legends could be made out under our paint.

"Maybe we can finish this up tonight," said

Jack, hopefully. "It's lucky you two had the time to get all these boxes and stuff. I didn't get off until late."

"I'm going to have lots of time from now on," said Simon grimly. "Dad wants me to quit my summer job."

"What for?" asked Jack.

"He thinks my Spanish is suffering."

"What are you going to do?"

"Quit my summer job. What else can I do? After turning cartwheels over at Sears to convince them how reliable I was, I have to go in and tell them I quit."

"They won't have any trouble finding someone else, anyway," said Jack.

"Oh, I know."

Silence.

I thought this sounded incredibly high-handed of Simon's father. I couldn't imagine my own father taking that sort of tack no matter how nutty he was about Spanish. And if he did, I couldn't imagine that Jack or I would so quietly give in. But it was becoming more evident to me every minute that I didn't understand the workings of Simon's family.

We did a very neat job of covering the boxes with brown paper, but Simon didn't seem to be enjoying himself much. He was obviously unhappy about having to quit his job. I thought about how much easier life would be if people just drifted along enjoying life instead of worrying about their Spanish or getting enough cardboard boxes. I watched the lamplight cast a faint shadow on Simon's cheekbone.

"'Gather ye rosebuds while ye may,'" I murmured.

"What did you say, Brenna?" said Jack.

"What a day!" I said quickly.

Jack looked at me suspiciously. "Where's the paint?" he asked. "Aren't we supposed to be making these things look like dogs?"

I jumped. "Right. I've got the paint right here." I pulled some bottles of brown, black, and white tempera out of the kitchen cupboard.

Simon said we'd better sketch in our plan first with pencil to avoid mistakes and the consequent necessity to recover the boxes. He took a pencil and with intense concentration began to draw a dog's nose on his box. "It's been nice," he said, "having some money of my own from the Sears job."

"But your Dad sends you enough money," said Jack.

"Yeah, but it was better having my own." Simon stood away a bit to scrutinize his dog's penciled nose, then meditatively started to sketch it a bit larger. "The thing about taking money from Dad," he said, "is that it has a way of making you feel like a slave or something."

Ah, I noted, the let-'em-eat-cake manner runs in the family. I tried to imagine what Simon's father was like but only came up with the idea of someone along the lines of the giant in *Jack and the Beanstalk,* but in a three piece suit.

I had never heard Simon come out with so much personal information at once, but he was obviously in a reflective mood. "I guess Mom could have put the screws to Dad in the divorce court," he said, reaching slowly for a brush, "but she'd rather not have to take his money." He shrugged. "Oh, I don't know. How many of these boxes do we have to do?"

It took us quite a while to get the boxes painted to look like dogs. Simon finished his two first and sat back with a Coke to watch Jack and me work. If I had expected to be the subject of such scrutiny I would have dressed more carefully. As it was, my hair was pulled back in a rubber band and I was wearing last year's blue jeans. But it was too late now to do anything but hold my stomach in, so I concentrated intently on that.

"You should always wear jeans, Brenna," said Simon, obviously mellowed by the Coke.

Jack chortled. "She certainly should, seeing as how she's always up to her ears in dog dip."

I shot him a look. My ears were burning. Could it be that Simon really liked me? After all, why not? He liked Jack and although I am only half Jack's size, we are related. I concentrated on painting the tail of my doggy box. Anyone who could like Jack could like anybody, I thought fiercely.

"That's it for me," said Jack, sticking his paintbrush into the jar of water and heading for the refrigerator. "Who wants a nice salami sand-wich?"

Thinking of what he had already packed in his stomach at suppertime, I suppressed a shudder. If I ever got married, I intended to start saving at the outset for the years when I would be feeding a teenaged boy.

"I'll have one," said Simon.

When I finished painting my last box, I took a Coke to the chair where the lamp casts a shadow so I could quit worrying about holding in my stomach. I sat there for a minute thinking I was glad I wasn't in Simon's position. The better I got to know Simon, the less he seemed like the Lord High Executioner and the more he was like a regular person with ordinary worries. His father didn't sound as if he'd be much fun to have around. I could see now how he happened to have the snazzy car while he and his mother lived in a dinky house. It was fairly unpleasant when you thought about it. It certainly is nicer if a family is all chummy and together—like my family.

"You know," I said suddenly, "it's been ages since Mom and Dad have been on me about not having direction to my life, not working towards a goal and all that."

"With you running around all over the place putting up notices, making dog boxes, and dipping dogs, they probably think it would sound a little silly to tell you to get busy," said Simon, amused.

I had been rather busy lately, I admitted to

myself. Not that it was work exactly. But that train of thought reminded me of all we still had to get done. "Something else we need to think about," I said, "is vet bills. That puppy hasn't even had its puppy shots."

"We can make little wooden boxes for cash donations," suggested Jack, "and put them at the convenience stores, the library, and places like that, but I know we're mostly going to get small change."

"I'll give you your first donation," said Simon, grandly. "Thirty dollars of Dad's money."

"Gee, thanks, Simon," I said. "That's awfully nice of you. Maybe I'll go ahead and take the puppy in tomorrow." I hesitated a minute. "What do you think of my talking to Dr. Briggs and seeing if he'd be willing to donate a little of his time to the society. Do you think he might do it?"

"It won't do any harm to ask," said Simon.

I wasted no time the next day taking the puppy in to see Dr. Briggs. It was hard to nerve myself to ask if he would donate some time to the Dog Protection Society. The thing I disliked most about this whole enterprise was asking people to help out. But there was no way out of it. This just wasn't something a person could do single-handedly.

While he peered into the puppy's mouth, prodded her tummy, and gave her the required shots, I filled him in on the history and aims of the Dog

Protection Society. "The fact is," I concluded, "we need someone who would be willing to give some free time and advice if the dogs need vetting. The society may be able to pay something, but I'm not sure how much because we haven't got our fundraising underway yet." I did not think this was the time to explain that our fundraising so far consisted of a set of little wooden boxes which were still in the planning stage.

"We-ell," he said. "I don't know. Why don't you get back to me as the thing solidifies. Maybe I could help out a little. You know, you can do some of the work yourself. It's not like with people. There's no law against practicing medicine on animals without a license. Dog breeders do a lot of the routine maintenance on their animals themselves."

At least he hadn't actually said no, I thought, as I gathered up the puppy to leave.

The time came to test Dr. Briggs' good will sooner than I expected. The next day dawned muggy and gloomy. By noon it was pouring down rain, complete with lightening and crashing sound effects. In the midst of all this high theater, my old Sunday school teacher, Mrs. Spooner, called. Mrs. Spooner was old when I was in Sunday school and she's gotten a lot older since. I was amazed that she called because Mrs. Spooner is the sort of person who worries a lot about being electrocuted by the telephone—she's more than a little timid. I felt uneasy myself hearing the static crackle on the line.

"Brenna," she said, her voice quavery, "I saw your box for the dogs this morning in the A&P and I gave you a can of dog food."

Our campaign is working, I thought with satisfaction. I didn't ask myself how Mrs. Spooner knew that I was the moving force of the Dog Protection Society. News travels fast in Oakdale.

"I wonder if you can help me," she went on. "A dog has been lying in my front yard since yesterday and still hasn't moved. Don't you think that's strange? It hasn't moved since I first noticed it yesterday afternoon and it's lying out there now in all this rain. Something must be wrong with it."

"Could it be dead?" I inquired delicately.

A spasm of static cracked along the line. "Oh, no, it's not dead," she assured me, "but I'm afraid to go near it."

So am I, I thought. But I said, "I'll see what we can do, Mrs. Spooner. I'm not sure we can help, but I'll get back to you."

After I hung up, I felt a sudden panic. What could I do? There is something decidedly alarming about an animal acting strange. You may not know what is going to happen, but as long as its biting you is one of the possibilities, you can't help but feel uneasy. The first thing I thought of was to call Sergeant Mulhoney. When you're afraid, I reasoned, you call a policeman. Unfortunately, it turned out that Sergeant Mulhoney was away for the day at a law enforcement workshop.

I explained my problem to Judy, the police dispatcher and secretary.

"Sergeant Mulhoney always handles these cases," she said nasally. "He'll be back tomorrow."

But I need him now, I thought. Now. Then I had an idea. "What does Sergeant Mulhoney do when he goes out on one of these cases?" I inquired.

Judy thought. The thunder crashed outside and the telephone protested. "Well, he takes his gun," she said helpfully. "And he puts on his leather jacket and helmet and leather gloves. I think he worries about being bitten."

No kidding, I thought. "I'm going to need to borrow the helmet and leather jacket," I said. "I'll be by to pick them up in the next half hour." I'm sure I could never have gotten away with borrowing police equipment in New York City, but then Oakdale is not New York.

My next phone call was to Simon. I felt funny about it, but I had to be sensible. Nobody else was available, and if I were attacked by a mad dog, I would certainly need someone to drive me to the hospital.

He answered the phone on the first ring, and I quickly outlined the situation. "I'm feeling so low after quitting my job," he said, "that bringing in a sick dog almost sounds like fun to me. Sure, I'll do it."

When I pulled up in front of Simon's house a few minutes later, I started to get out and politely ring the doorbell, but watching the rain beat against my windshield, I reconsidered and blew the horn. Simon came running out, flung open the car door, and jumped in. He was wearing a blue windbreaker but was, of course, soaked. The rain ran in tiny rivulets down his black eyebrows. He shook droplets out of his hair, twisted around, and threw the old blanket he was carrying into the back seat. "We'll need something to carry him in," he explained. The car seemed considerably warmer now that Simon was in it. The windows were fogging and I had to open mine a crack and wipe off the windshield with a handkerchief. Drops of water blew in through the window.

I slowly and carefully made my way to the police station then we each opened our doors and dashed up the front steps to the entrance. Once we stepped in we were hit by the full force of the air conditioning on all our wetness. I shuddered. Modern conveniences can almost be the death of you. "I've come to get all that leather stuff of Sergeant Mulhoney's," I said, teeth chattering. Judy looked Simon up and down approvingly. "Oh, a *guy* is going to do it," she said, with palpable relief.

That annoyed me, but one thing I'd already learned since I started the society was that I couldn't afford to speak sharply to anybody because I never knew when I'd need to be asking them for a favor. Who could have foreseen I would need help from all the grocery managers in town, from Dr. Briggs, and now even from Judy Shobless? So I just smiled sweetly and we walked out a few minutes later carrying pounds and pounds of leather protection.

The rain was still coming down steadily when we pulled up in front of Mrs. Spooner's neat little white house. Lying under an oak in front of her house was the dog. His head was up and he was breathing, but it was certainly very strange that he hadn't moved to shelter. Bumping my elbow against the car window, I struggled to put on Sergeant Mulhoney's helmet. Unfortunately, I discovered that it dropped down over my eyes, obscuring my vision considerably.

"Hey, what are you up to?" said Simon. "I'm the one that's going to get the dog."

"I didn't expect you to get the dog," I explained. "I just brought you along to drive me to the hospital if the dog attacks me."

Simon laughed mirthlessly. "I can see myself explaining to Jack that I sent you out to be attacked by a mad dog." He began putting on the leather jacket, no easy task in the hot, muggy confines of our little car. It was embarrassing to have to conform to Judy Shobless' ideas of the sexual division of labor, but I gave in and handed over the helmet.

"What should I do if it attacks you?" I said weakly.

"That's a problem all right," he said. He got out of the car. The rain streamed down the helmet and the leather jacket. "I don't think it's going to happen though," he said, raising his voice to be heard above the rain. "He might bite, but I think if he could move, he would have moved already."

I rubbed a clear space on the foggy window and peered out, watching nervously as Simon moved slowly towards the dog. I noticed that at the front window of the house the white curtains had parted. Mrs. Spooner was also peeking. It was like a scene from the movie *High Noon*. Simon moved cautiously, holding the folded blanket before him. The dog looked up at him but did not move away. I tried to remember what I had heard about subduing dogs. The only thing I could recall was that you were supposed to turn a hose on them. Ha! A lot of good that would do on a day like today.

Simon knelt next to the dog. I could see he was tucking the blanket around it. Then he picked it up and walked back to the car. The poor thing didn't even struggle. I leaned over and opened the car door. Raindrops darkened on the upholstery as Simon lay the dog on the floor of the back seat. It was a medium-sized mutt, its wet coat darkly glued to it in clumps. It looked at me sadly. "Poor dog," I said. "Poor, poor dog." Simon slid in beside me, closed the door, and wiggled out of the leather jacket. "Where to now?" he said. Limp with relief that no blood had been spilled, I switched on the ignition. "To Dr. Briggs."

I drove right up on the sidewalk in front of Dr. Briggs' office. Simon lifted the dog and, hunched over against the rain, carried him into the office. I followed close on his heels, sloshing through the streaming water at the office's front door.

Dr. Briggs was sitting at the receptionist's desk reading *Veterinary World*. I unbuttoned my raincoat and breathed deeply. "I have a charity case for you," I said.

"Oh, you do, do you," he said amiably. A young woman with straggly hair appeared, dressed in a white coat. She deftly whipped the dog up and carried it to the examination table. We followed her in. I figured so far so good. Dr. Briggs hadn't said yes, but he hadn't said no either.

"Tick paralysis," Dr. Briggs announced.

"Tick paralysis?" I repeated. "What does that mean?"

"It means that when we get the ticks off him he's going to be fine," said Dr. Briggs briskly. "You can leave him here overnight and pick him up tomorrow."

I couldn't believe it. A happy ending. Simon shook hands ceremonially with Dr. Briggs. I thanked him on behalf of the Dog Protection Society, then we made our way out through the waiting room to the car on the sidewalk. I slid damply behind the wheel.

"How about that!" said Simon. "I was afraid that one was a goner."

"It didn't look good," I agreed, starting up the car. Now that everything had turned out all right, I could concentrate on how nice it was to have Simon in the car with me, to have him so pleasantly close and cozy. I wondered if he were pleased to be cozily close to me, the windows all foggy and blurred with rain. But it didn't seem likely. If he did feel that way he would have done something to show it—kiss me or ask me to a movie or something. I took myself in hand and turned my mind to a more rational subject, the problems of running the Dog Protection Society. There, at least, was something I could do something about.

"You know," I said, "what we've got to work on is finding some permanent homes for the dogs. We keep getting dogs and getting dogs, but we never get rid of any of them. Unless we can do better, we'll soon be in the soup.

"Maybe our classified ads don't have enough sizzle in them," I continued. "I got a call yesterday about the puppy, but I haven't had a single nibble on the other dogs. What do you think about adding photos to the notices on the community bulletin boards?"

"I don't know," said Simon. "We've got a problem all right. We've got to come up with something a lot better than what we've been doing. A lot better." His eyebrows seemed to straighten out under the pressure of worry.

I felt a little wave of relief that I wasn't the only

one doing the worrying. I was glad for help making donation boxes, and I knew I was lucky to be able to call on Simon in an emergency like today, but all this paled before the relief of sharing the worrying. The Dog Protection Society was a big responsibility, that was for sure.

5

Before I even went by Dr. Briggs' to pick up the dog we had rescued from Mrs. Spooner's yard the day before, I got on the phone to try to find a place for it to stay. I wanted to save the farm kids we had lined up for large and active dogs, so I called my friend Janey.

"I could keep it just temporarily, I guess," she said, "particularly if you pick up the tab for the food, but the thing is, we're going on vacation next month."

"Fine," I said heartily. I had decided to take advantage of every answer that wasn't a flat no.

My idea was to get people committed inch by inch.

Janey immediately began having second thoughts. "Uh . . ." she began.

"I'll bring him by sometime this afternoon," I said hastily, hanging up.

The dog was walking around when I picked him up at Dr. Briggs', but that was just about all you could say for him. Here was a dog without looks or personality, poor thing. Instead of taking him straight to Janey's, I took him home so I could bathe and groom him. I even poured some of my own hair conditioner into the final rinse water. "Help for limp, dry hair," it said on the label. I had hopes it would give him the same golden glow that you saw on the lovely blonde pictured on the box; I wanted Janey to have a positive attitude towards him.

He dried quickly in the afternoon sun and I brushed him for a good while. I was disappointed to see that he looked pretty much the same as before. Still, he did smell good.

Janey has a big yard. She used to have a Great Dane, but it had died a couple of months before, and her family was still so upset they weren't considering getting another dog. "Nobody could replace Sweet Pea," Janey had sniffled to me. I knew that Janey was good and conscientious about dogs, but after the regal presence of Sweet Pea I was afraid the sight of this dog might prove a bit of a shock. I fluffed up his hair a bit with the blow drier before I set out, and hoped for the best.

"Is that it?" Janey said dubiously when we arrived. "Goodness, it's small." It was not particularly small at all, but Great Dane owners have a peculiar standard.

I lifted the bag of dog food out of the car. "It's had a hard time," I said. "It needs a lot of love and understanding." Facing that I had failed to improve the dog's looks, I had decided the best approach would be to appeal to her better nature.

"It can have all the love and understanding it needs until next month," said Janey.

This kind of response from my friend the animal lover gave me momentary qualms about the future of the Dog Protection Society, but it was too late now to be fainthearted. We took the dog into Janey's backyard, the ground squishy under our feet after yesterday's rain. Then we sat down on the back steps together and watched it hesitantly sniff its way around.

"Has it eaten yet?" asked Janey.

"I don't know."

"Maybe we'd better give him a little something. It might make him feel more at home."

We went inside where Janey could simmer some chicken livers to add appeal to the dry dog food. When she dropped a bouillon cube into the livers to enhance their flavor, I quit worrying about how the stray would fare here. The dog lover in Janey was slowly rising to the fore even with this most unpromising subject.

Because of my preoccupation with the dogs, it had been ages since I had talked to Janey. "How's the job at the day care?" I asked.

"It's taken a little getting used to," admitted Janey. "I come home absolutely pooped but the kids are great. And since it's only in the mornings, I have the afternoon for swimming." She blushed. "I've done a little sailing, too."

"I didn't know your family had bought a boat," I said, surprised.

"We haven't. Gary is teaching me on his family's boat. You know Gary Potter."

Of course I knew Gary Potter. Hadn't I been expecting a phone call any day now from him as soon as he got back from the Grand Canyon?

"Oh, they're back from vacation?" I said with studied indifference.

"They've been back for weeks," said Janey. "They loved the Grand Canyon. Rode all over the place on burros, took lots of pictures. Of course, Gary's not very keen on scenery."

Apparently, Gary wasn't too keen on me either, I thought sadly. A bit of sailing would have been a nice break from brushing dogs.

"I guess he liked the burros, though," I said, nobly trying to keep up my side of the conversation.

"Yes, loved the burros." Janey took the livers off the stove and began to chop them up, her back to me. "Brenna, you aren't annoyed about Gary are you?"

"Oh, no," I said. "There was nothing between

Gary and me." The second part of this statement, at least, was true.

"I knew you had been out with him some, so I was a little worried."

"There wasn't anything to that," I said. "We just went to a couple of movies together. Put it out of your mind. You really like him, huh?"

Janey turned, holding the bowl full of chopped chicken livers, and looked dreamily into the distance. She said, "He's not like other boys. He's a thinker. A deep person."

This was a side of Gary that had completely eluded me. I would have said he had no distinguishing personal characteristics at all except for a fondness for milk shakes. Clearly he and Janey were made for each other. I had to try to rise to the occasion and be a good friend.

"It's great that he's found someone to really understand and appreciate him," I said loyally.

"Oh, I do appreciate him, I do," she breathed.

It was hard to descend gracefully from this plane to chicken livers, but next we mixed the livers well into the dog food and presented the concoction to the dog who was outside looking uneasily this way and that. At first he appeared to wonder whether this heavenly dish was intended for him. We murmured encouragement. "That's right, cutie, it's for you," I assured him. He began to nibble at it.

Janey regarded him sympathetically. "I wonder if you'll be able to find a home for him. The poor thing doesn't have much going for him." I looked at him and for an unnerving instant felt a flash of kinship with that poor dog. There was no logical reason why I should be feeling like a stray mutt just because neither Gary nor Simon chose to ask me out. Nevertheless, I could feel depression sweeping over me. I got up briskly and dusted my hands on my pants. I decided I'd better get moving before I sank to that even lower state of mind in which I wished I were a guinea pig.

As I drove away from Janey's house, the thick trees and solid houses of Northgreen Lane seemed to dissolve, and while I was careful to follow the traffic signals and drive soberly on, in a corner of my mind was a sailboat. Its orange sails had fat bellies as it scudded playfully across a blue lagoon. Since I don't have any idea how to sail, the part of the daydream where I was capably pulling at various ropes about the boat was a bit vague, but I was clear about one thing—Simon was there beside me, completely besotted with me. I sighed with pleasure and turned the vision over in my mind as if toasting it evenly. Simon's warm hands were at my waist. He was looking nobly into the distance towards the sunset. No, he was looking deep into my eyes with a smile—that was much better.

A horn blew and an irritable matron in a station wagon passed me. The trees of Oakdale materialized again, but the vision left a pleasant afterglow.

In real life, however, I could see that the situation with Simon and me was not so promising. Girls are continually complaining, "What can I do to make him notice me?" And there is help for girls with this problem. There are lots of things you can do to make a boy notice you—drop your pencil, lose ten pounds, win the starring role in *Romeo and Juliet*. But there is nothing whatever you can do if he notices you but just isn't interested.

I tried to ask myself dispassionately if there was room for hope. I felt the most promising thing he had said so far was "You should always wear jeans." That was definitely favorable mention. Of course, he could have meant, as Jack said, that you should always wear jeans if you are going to spend your time dipping dogs, but it hadn't sounded like that. It had sounded like a compliment. On the other hand, I had to admit it was an isolated occurrence.

I pulled up in our driveway and got out, wondering if there were any health hazards to repeated showering. My jeans and me were distinctly doggy after my ministrations to the ugly-duckling dog. As luck would have it, Simon chose this time to pull up in front of the house in his snazzy red car.

He called to me, "Hey, Brenna." I turned. He had gotten out of the car and was leaning on the door. "I'm working on our problem about getting the dogs adopted. I think I've got an idea that will work."

Someone was in the car with him. I walked

closer, trying to peek into the car discreetly. "What kind of idea?" I asked. After a brief internal debate, I decided I was doggy enough that it would be unwise to get too close.

"I don't want to tell you now because I haven't got it definitely set up, and it might not work out," he said, "but I saw you outside and couldn't resist letting you know I was working on it. Have you met Margarita?"

After that, of course, I had to go over to him and make friendly noises to the person in the car. This was a mixed blessing. On the one hand, it meant I got a very good look at Margarita. On the other hand, what I saw made me feel ill.

Margarita smiled at me. She was beautiful. Flawless skin, liquid eyes, clouds of dark hair, tiny delicate waist. She looked like a South American Barbie doll, only more overdone. "Hello, Brenna," she said sweetly.

I trust I did not bare my fangs and snarl at the girl, but what I actually did do is a bit of a blur. Even from a slight distance I could tell Margarita favored perfume. Not to my taste exactly, but far superior to the smells I was exuding, a mixture of dogginess and flea powder.

"I'd better get Margarita back to the dorm," said Simon. "I'll let you know as soon as anything's definite."

I smiled and waved as they drove off. "Oh, *do* take Margarita back to the dorm," I cooed to myself as they drove out of sight, "and please wring her neck for me." I don't know what got into me. As a rule I am a gentle person.

A couple of evenings later Simon called Jack. "Simon has a great new idea," Jack reported to me. "He'll be over in a few minutes to tell us about it." So Simon had a great idea. Did he have to keep it under wraps until now? Couldn't he ask to speak to me for a change? Couldn't I at least be thrown the crumb of being treated like a real person?

My hopes were so dulled I didn't even switch into jeans for Simon's arrival but left on the sundress I had bought—oh, irony—when planning my fun, fun summer. I stood before the full-length mirror in it and compared myself point by point with Margarita. Fortunately, I had the good sense to put an end to this self-torture and when Simon arrived I was sitting quite composedly, my skirt spread out on the couch, reading the evening newspaper. He and Jack came into the room laughing about something.

"Wait till you hear what Simon's been up to," crowed Jack.

I regarded them with the composure of the young Queen Victoria, but no one seemed to notice.

"I didn't like to tell you about it until I had it all set up," said Simon, throwing himself in a chair, "but—we're going to advertise the dogs on television."

"But Simon," I protested feebly, "we can't do that. It would cost a fortune."

He held up his hand. "Wait. Public service spot. The station is going to give us five minutes on Saturday mornings—free."

Jack stretched his long legs and arms out on the couch and waxed ecstatic. "That's fantastic. Isn't that fantastic, Brenna. How did you ever do it? Boy, I can't get over it. That is positively great."

"Actually," said Simon, savoring his triumph but wishing to appear modest, "I got some help from Elwood Curtis."

"The mayor?" I said.

"Of course, the mayor, dum-dum," said Jack witheringly. "How many Elwood Curtises can there be around here?"

"And I think it was a help, too, that I know the station manager," said Simon. "He knows Dad. Then it was lucky that they were actually looking for a public service spot to do."

"You deserve a lot of the credit," said Jack.

"Well, I did make a short, snappy presentation for them about how it would be entertaining as well as a public service," said Simon smugly.

"I don't quite see how it's going to work," I said. "What will we *do* on the public service spot?"

"We will just show the dogs," said Simon. "What television has done for toothpaste it can do for us."

"Simon's right," said Jack. "Think of how

people are always writing love letters to TV stars, proposing marriage and all. People have this magnetic attraction to anything they see on the tube. All you have to do is show it to them and they crave it."

I could see he might have a point. And after all, the TV spot was free. "Maybe you're right," I said, warming to the idea. "It's a fantastic opportunity." I sat up straight. "I think besides showing the dogs we should say a few words about any special needs they have. We want to settle them in homes where they will fit in. Big dogs to families with big yards, and so forth. Do you think it would be better to showcase just one dog at a time? Or more?"

"I think you can do up to three at a time," said Simon, "if you talk fairly fast. Now you're going to need to wear something simple."

"Me?" I squealed. "Why me? I thought you were going to do it."

Simon gave Jack a look. I could see they had already talked about it between themselves.

"But you have all that drama club experience," said Jack persuasively.

If you didn't count the time I played one of the Three Little Pigs in first grade, my on-stage experience was limited to playing the third witch in *Macbeth* last year. My lines on that occasion had been: "That will be ere the set of sun. . . . There to meet with Macbeth. . . . anon!" I had been particularly proud of my "Anon!", not an easy line to carry off, but I didn't see that this experience would be of any help in the present instance.

"But that was mostly painting scenery," I said. "I've never been on television."

"You'll be fine," said Simon. "Jack will help you practice, won't you, Jack? The important thing is to get your timing down pat. You want it to run exactly five minutes."

I sat there feeling slightly stupefied.

"Look, Brenna, you want to get the dogs adopted, don't you?" said Simon. "I'm sure you're the best one for the job. Now Jack here would be happy to do it, but look at him. Would you buy a used car from this man?"

Simon gave Jack a shove and they both laughed. I did not. I felt too sick to my stomach to join in the general gaiety of the occasion. I could already feel the cold eye of the camera on me. Then I had an even more horrible thought. What if when the camera panned toward me, while the eyes of the world were fixed upon me, I began to hiccup?

6

The only bright spot in the week that followed was the dog-dipping basin Simon made in his yard. I saw it Wednesday when I went over to his house to pick up some of the dog food Simon had gathered from the donation boxes. When I got there I found him surrounded by empty bags of Sakrete, smoothing off the wet surface of this cement-lined pit. I looked at him in amazement.

"Don't look at me that way, Brenna," he said uneasily. "I can't work on Spanish *all* the time."

"I was just wondering what you're doing. It looks great, but what is it?"

"It's a dog-dipping pit. You just fill it with dip and all you have to do is walk the dog in and presto—death to fleas."

Automated dipping. What an idea! No more picking up a squirming guest dog and throwing him into the washtub. In my eyes, the square cement hole began to glow with the seraphic beauty of Michelangelo's marble.

"It'll have a heavy, weighted cover when I finish," he went on, "for safety. And you see this graduated decline so you can walk the dog down? I'm roughing it up so their feet will have a secure grip. The only trouble is, I wasn't able to fix up a real drain, so we're going to have to siphon it dry when we change the dip."

"It's beautiful," I said warmly. "But I'm surprised your mother let you."

"Well, she wasn't too keen, but it's over to the side here and sunken, so it won't show much. I told her that when we quit using it, I'd fill it in and plant geraniums in it for her."

That was a sharp reminder to me that the dark days would come when Simon and Jack had gone away to college and wouldn't be around to help out at all. A bleak thought.

Simon brushed cement dust off his hands. "Come on and let me get that dog food for you. I'd better get washed up. I've got to pick up Margarita in a little while."

Pick up Margarita? It did seem unfair that I didn't even have time to gloat over the dog-dipping pit before being hit with a double whammy, but I carried on valiantly, following Simon to the garage to get the dog food.

"I just hope that cement doesn't crack," he said. "I've never done anything as big as that before."

We carried a couple of five-pound bags of dog food out to the car. "How's the television commercial coming?" he asked.

"Okay. I'm practicing in front of the mirror."

"Will you be ready in time?" he asked anxiously. "You've only got two more days to practice."

"Of course," I said. "Remember all my drama club experience."

He had the grace to look uncomfortable.

"Why don't I plan to drive you to the TV station," he said. "I know where the station is and I can help you with the dogs."

"Okay," I said. I seemed to have lost much of my usual interest in life since I had heard the name Margarita.

"I think we'd better leave good and early," he said. "I hate to think how I'd face Mr. Eliot if we got a flat tire and didn't make it in time."

"Okay," I said. My cares weighed heavily on me. In fact, I felt bent over like a croquet hoop.

Simon loaded the bags into the trunk for me and as I drove away gave the fender a friendly pat of farewell. All right for him, I thought bitterly. He wasn't having to make a television appearance.

That television spot was like a blight of frost on

my life. The most innocent pleasures dissolved instantly at its touch. When I got home from Simon's I pulled out the pruning shears and started trimming the vibernum hedge in the backyard. The lines of the hedge were becoming steadily more square, the bees were buzzing on the spiky white vibernum blossoms, and I was feeling nicely sun warmed when suddenly I thought of the television spot and got goosebumps all over. That sort of thing was happening to me all the time lately. I finally had come to understand what was meant by the expression "It made my blood run cold." Since the TV spot had been planned my blood was as chilled as your average Coca-Cola.

Shivering, I dropped the pruning shears, went in, and tuned in to a television quiz show, a morbid habit I had recently acquired. But I couldn't take more than a few minutes of the contestants' nervous giggles before I switched the set off, stifling a groan. It was clear to me that the average person thrust under the glare of the television camera did not react with the poise of Walter Cronkite. I knew I was going to look like an idiot.

I went to my bedroom and smiled brightly at the mirror. "I'm Brenna Matthews speaking for Oakdale's Dog Protection Society. I'd like to introduce you to some of my friends who need a good home." I looked at my white teeth reflected in the mirror. Would you take a used dog from this girl? Probably not.

That evening, it occurred to me that I really should practice with the dogs. Practicing alone in front of my mirror didn't simulate the real event closely enough. I unhitched the hall mirror and took it out to the backyard with me, propping it up against a lawn chair.

"Brenna," Mom called from the back door, "What are you doing out there with the hall mirror?"

"Practicing for the TV," I called back.

"Well, don't let the dogs gnaw on the mirror, please."

That evening's practice with the dogs was discouraging, but useful. I saw at once that my best linen suit wouldn't do for the TV after all. I needed something that wouldn't show paw prints at the first doggy onslaught. I also needed something that would protect my shins from eager scratchings. Yelps of pain from me could only discourage a prospective owner. Looking at it from that point of view, I knew at once what the perfect outfit would be. But did I really want to appear in front of all those folks out there in television land in my ragged jeans and an old Snoopy sweatshirt?

Thursday and Friday seemed to drag painfully by. How I looked forward to having Saturday over and done with. How I would dance and sing once I was through with this ordeal! Presuming I survived it.

*   *   *

When Saturday morning finally dawned, I could tell at once by the sick feeling in my stomach exactly what day it was. I slouched over to the dressing table mirror and gave it a bright smile.

"I'm Brenna Matthews," I said. It seemed to me I had an unfortunate resemblance to my father as he usually appears in the morning, a look of fish-eyed pain. I turned quickly away from the mirror, and pulling a bathrobe around me, staggered down the hall and into the kitchen.

Jack was sitting at the bar eating bacon, sausages, fried eggs, and orange juice with a side order of potatoes. "So this is the big day, huh, old girl," he said heartily, shovelling eggs into his mouth.

I felt decidedly woozy.

"What would you like for breakfast, dear," Mother inquired solicitously.

"A little dry toast, maybe," I said.

"Why don't I poach you a nice egg and you could have a little juice," Mom said. "You need your vitamins."

"Better not make her eat," advised Jack cheerfully. "She might throw up."

I sat down and held my head up with my hands. "Just dry toast," I said.

"Is it all fixed what you're going to say?" said Jack.

Another cold spasm ran through my stomach.

"Jack, quit talking about it," said Mom sharply, "until she has a little food in her stomach."

When the toast appeared, I chewed it very slowly, pretending I was some ruminating animal like a cow, or a camel, some placid creature who just put one foot in front of another all its life and never had to go on television.

Jack was regarding me with bright-eyed interest. "Don't you think you've chewed it enough?" he asked.

"Leave her alone, Jack," said Mom. "If you can't control yourself you can take your plate into the dining room."

"I wasn't doing anything," he protested, popping a strip of bacon into his mouth.

"I don't want you to rush, dear," said Mother, "but Simon called earlier and you need to keep in mind that he'll be picking you up at nine-thirty."

"Nine-thirty!" I cried in panic. "It isn't going to take us two hours to drive to Rock Ridge!"

"He wants to allow time for every eventuality," said Mom. "This will give you time to compose your thoughts after you arrive."

Galvanized, I jumped up stiffly and headed back to my room.

"Don't forget your juice, Brenna," called Mom. "You need your vitamins."

In my room, I pulled on my most rumple-proof, smudge-proof brown corderoy pants, then brushed my hair, which at least was shining and clean. Next I ran out back to check on the dogs. I had fetched the beagle from Tony Harris' place yesterday and had carefully bathed and brushed all three prospective adoptees. Now, theoretically, all I had to do was snap leashes on their collars and walk them sedately to Simon's car, but unaccountably, I felt uneasy. When I went out to check on them I could see Guest Dog, Puppy, and Clown Dog lying down together near the hollyhocks in the morning sun. But where was the beagle? Could he have gotten out some how? I scanned the perimeters of the fence. Then I saw him. Or to be more accurate, I saw a brown tail bobbing around under an azalea bush; that was all that could be seen of the beagle, who otherwise was hidden in a hole of impressive depth. The azalea, its moorings weakened, wobbled a little.

"Jack," I screeched, "Jack, come help me!" I ran to the scene of the crime. When I skidded to a stop at the azalea bush, the beagle's face appeared, smiling powerfully. His wagging tail caused the tottering azalea to quiver.

Jack was soon at my side, panting. "What's wrong."

"Looooook," I keened. "Look how *filthy* he is!"

Jack looked down. "Wow, that is one heck of a hole," he said.

"I am not interested in your admiring the dog's engineering prowess," I said acidly. "We've got to get him cleaned up and I'm already wearing my good clothes."

Jack swiftly made a grab for the beagle and got him by the loose scruff of his neck. "Gotcha, you little devil," he said. "Good grief, he really is a mess. I think we better throw him in the bathtub." Dripping clods of dirt at every step, he progressed towards the back door.

At that moment, Simon came up to the back gate. "Hey, Brenna, are you ready?"

"We have had a slight mishap," I said.

"Crikey!" said Simon, noticing the beagle for the first time. "He really is a mess, isn't he!" Dirt was caked on the beagle's nose and decorated his eyelashes.

"I'll just dump him in the bathtub," said Jack. "He can dry during the drive."

Mother normally wouldn't have favored bathing a dog in the bathtub, but understanding the urgency of the situation, she did nothing but stand aside and made tut-tutting noises. I leaned weakly against a wall, awaiting Jack and Simon's reappearance with the cleaned up beagle.

"Your father had to go to work early, Brenna," Mom said, drying her hands on her apron, "but he's going to make a special trip home at eleven-thirty to see you on TV."

I was surprised to note that the word TV did not cause a nauseous wave to pass over me. The fact was that I now felt calmer. Since we had fished the beagle out of the dirt, I had realized that it was the dogs that were important, not me. It was the dogs that the camera would be focused on. It was the dogs who needed to be clean, well-brushed, and charming. When I clung to that thought, I felt calmer. Not *perfectly* calm, you understand, but calmer.

When Jack appeared, holding the unrepentant

beagle in a bath towel, I even managed a sickly smile. Simon glanced at his watch. "Good thing I allowed plenty of time," he said. "You go get in the car, Brenna. I'll get the other two dogs."

It would have been nice if he'd said I looked fine. It would have been pleasant even to be looked at at all, but I was too busy rehearsing my lines to myself to brood over that. I sat quietly in the bucket seat, saying nervously, "My name is Brenna Matthews," until Simon appeared and dropped the puppy in my lap. Together he and Jack tied the beagle's and the clown dog's leashes to the seat belts in the back and cracked a back window so the beagle would be dried by the breeze as we drove.

Mother blew me a kiss as we pulled out of the driveway. "You'll be great," she called. "You look terrific."

A girl can count on her mother.

We drove out past the Northgreen Shopping Center and then pulled out on the highway. Simon was whistling "Waltzing Matilda."

"Don't look so grim, Brenna," he said. "It's the dogs they'll be looking at, not you."

"That's just what I've been telling myself," I said. I flexed my rigid fingers and tried to make social chit chat. "How's the Spanish coming?"

Simon grinned. "So you're going to try to make a nervous wreck out of me, too," he said. He carefully looked behind him, then changed lanes. Now that I knew Simon better, I realized it was one of nature's little jokes that because he did

everything carefully he looked so piratical. "I'm
sure working on it enough," he said, "but Dad's
beginning to talk about how I really need to live
in a Spanish-speaking country and have total
immersion in the language."

"Oh?" I said, trying to achieve just the right
tone of polite interest while my heart sank to my
loafers. "What does he have in mind?"

"Seeing that I'm too old for summer camp, it's
a bit of a problem, but I think he's plotting for me
to live with the plant manager's family at a coffee
mill outside Santo Domingo."

"Is that definite?" I gulped.

"Oh, he hasn't actually put it to me yet. I'm just
guessing about what he has in mind going by a
couple of things he's said. He won't spring it on
me until he's got all the details worked out and
persuaded Mom to go along with it. He likes to
get all his ducks in a row, as he'd say."

"I guess it would be interesting to live in Santo
Domingo," I said heroically.

"It's nice," said Simon, "but Mom and I
haven't even been in Oakdale a year. I've just
gotten to know people. It doesn't make sense to
me that I should be picked up and sent off to
Santo Domingo."

"You've been rehearsing what to say to your
father when he pops it on you," I guessed.

"Yes," he admitted.

"Your father sounds kind of overbearing," I
ventured.

"He's all right. But you know what people are

like when they're doing things for your own good."

A sigh escaped me. I did indeed. "It would be so much nicer," I said, "if people just . . ." I wasn't sure exactly how to say what I meant but daisy chains, butterflies, and blueberry donuts swam before my eyes as I struggled to formulate my idea. Finally, to my relief, some words coalesced. ". . . lived for the moment," I finished triumphantly. I went on in a burst of poetry, "You know, 'Gather ye rosebuds while ye may, Old Time is still a-flying: And that same flower that smiles today, Tomorrow will be dying.' "

Simon looked at me in surprise. "But you can't be picking flowers all the time," he said.

"The principle is sound," I maintained stoutly. "Do you really like spending your whole summer working on Spanish?"

"I don't hate it, if that's what you mean. It's kind of like working with the dogs. It's a pain in the neck sometimes, but it's for a purpose, so that makes it different."

He had me there. I had to admit that all that work on the dogs wasn't exactly a bunch of roses, but I didn't mind doing it either. "Maybe I'll have to revise my philosophy of life to include the dogs," I conceded.

Simon grinned.

Outside, a haze of heat had begun to rise from the road and the fields, giving that landscape the lovely shimmery look that is one of the nice things about summer.

"Summer always reminds me of when I was little," said Simon. "Going barefoot and catching frogs. I was really happy back then."

"I didn't like being little," I said. "When you sat on the couch your feet didn't reach. Aren't you happy enough now?"

Simon shrugged. "Sure, but things are more complicated now. You do more thinking and catch fewer frogs."

I had the idea he was thinking about his parents, and I must have been right because after a few minutes silence he said, "It's the oddest thing. When you look at pictures of us back then we all look so happy."

"People generally look happy in pictures," I pointed out.

"Sure, but I think we really were happy. When people fall in love and get married, it stands to reason they're happy then, in the beginning. You tune in ten or fifteen years later and they can't stand each other. It's weird. People don't get to where they can't stand their kids after ten or fifteen years. Why do they get to where they can't stand each other?"

"It does happen with friends," I said. "In the fifth grade I used to be just crazy about this girl Becky, and in the sixth grade I couldn't stand her." But then I realized this wasn't really an intellectual discussion. I mean, I began to doubt that Simon was looking for an exhaustive analysis of human relationships. "It must be unsettling if it happens that way to your parents," I said.

For a few minutes neither of us spoke, then he said, "It's been a good summer anyway."

I didn't like the way he was speaking of it in the past tense. The nostalgic tone certainly suggested he was expecting to be sent over to the Dominican Republic any minute. I didn't want Simon to leave; I liked having him around. But I wanted more than that, too. I know I said that it was enough just to know he was there, like Sequoia National Park, but now I knew I wanted a closer relationship with Simon than I have with Sequoia National Park. Much closer.

At length we pulled up in the parking lot of the square brick television building and I began to feel the familiar qualm in my stomach.

"We've got plenty of time," Simon said. "I think we'd better walk the dogs."

Now that it was put to me, I could see it was most important that the dogs get the kinks out of their legs and seek out any necessary bushes and trees before they got on camera. I was lucky Simon could be trusted to think ahead. I took the happy-go-lucky clown dog and the puppy. Simon took the beagle, who was doing the great hunter bit, trying to hare off after rabbits in the woods. "Woooooooooouhooooooo," bayed the beagle. I recoiled. I hoped the studio was soundproof or everyone in eastern North Carolina was going to get the beagle's version of a call of the wild.

"That's enough of that," Simon said sharply to the beagle. "Pipe down." He snapped the beagle's leash and persuaded him to begin a prosaic circuit of the television building instead of setting off on a life rich in adventure in the nearby woods. I followed with the other two dogs at a distance calculated to remove them from the beagle's unsettling influence. We walked around the building once, then yet again. After the fourth circuit I said, "Maybe we'd better go in. Shouldn't we let them know we're here?"

Simon glanced at his watch. "Maybe so."

We made our way back to the front of the building and pushed our way through the heavy glass doors. As we stood just inside the front door, untangling dog leashes, a woman with tightly curled copper hair walked forward to meet us, smiling a receptionist-type smile. "You must be the . . ." she glanced at her notes, "Dog Protection Society." Bright smile. Her hair reminded me of one of those bunches of coiled wire you scrub pots with. "Let me show you where you can wait," she said sweetly. As we followed her down the dimly lit hallway, I noticed that even though she was bony, she was wearing a girdle. She had this sort of taut, springy look, like a jack-in-the-box. And a jack-in-the-box's smile, too. Lots of teeth.

She ushered us through the door of a waiting room furnished with black plastic chairs. The room was adorned only with a Coke machine, a clock, and three television screens. I have been in filling stations with more glamor. I wondered if it was like this behind stage everywhere. Hidden behind the glittering sets of opera and ballet and musical comedies, probably, there are rooms with black plastic chairs, old sponges, and cans of cleaning powder. The woman pivoted on her heel at the entrance to the room and, closing the door as she went, bowed out still smiling. I half expected her toothy smile to linger as the Cheshire cat's did, but to my relief she took it with her in the usual way.

"She certainly is a cheerful bugger," commented Simon. We were both finding our spirits a little oppressed by the ambience of the TV station. On the television screen we could watch Roger the Rodeo Clown, during whose cartoon show I was to appear. "And let's say happy birthday to all those boys and girls out there who had birthdays this week!" chirped Roger. Watching him, mesmerized, I began to feel I had never given enough credit to the people who appear on television. They may not say anything particularly amusing or bright, but on the other hand I had never seen a performer collapse into hysterical giggles. I was watching Roger's performance with admiration.

"Happy birthday! Happy birthday!" sang the television as the names of a hundred boys and girls rolled by.

I looked at the clock nervously. "How long would you say it will be until they call us?" I asked.

"I expect we've got a while, anyway," he said. "Do you think you can hold all three dogs while you're on camera, or had I better hand you the beagle at midpoint?"

"I think you'd better hand me the beagle. When I say, 'And now here's a very special little dog,' you hand him to me."

The beagle was weaving the leash around Simon, immobilizing him. "Hey, cut that out," he yelped. "I just hope I can move when the time comes," he said, unwinding the leash.

I led the dogs to the Coke machine and dropped in a coin.

"I don't think you'd better do that," said Simon as the coin clicked its way downward. "What if the Coke makes you burp?"

The Coke came down the chute with a clunk. I wordlessly handed it to Simon. "I wonder if there's a water fountain around here," I said longingly.

"I guess you'll have to ask old smile puss, keeper of the gate," he said gloomily.

Unnervingly close on the heels of this pronouncement, the woman with the smile appeared at the door to summon us. "We're almost ready for you," said the woman. "Jeanne will take you in and place you. When Roger has introduced you, Jeanne will give you your cue. Just remember to look at the camera with the red light."

The pallid young woman named Jeanne opened the door of the studio. It was a large barnlike room with a tangle of lights and cameras in the center. I could see on the far wall the model kitchen of "Good Cooking" and to the left of it the desks and weather map of the local evening news. Everything looked oddly detached. Then I realized that was because I was used to seeing the props neatly enclosed in the confines of the television screen. Roger the Rodeo Clown was on a platform at the far end of the long room, sitting on a tall stool in front of a collage of pictures of birthday cakes and presents. A boom microphone hovered over his head, beaming his words to kiddies for miles around, and three cameras pointed towards him. He was saying "And the top ten winners of our crayon contest will receive a Roger t-shirt with a picture on it of your old friend Roger."

Jeanne positioned me and showed Simon where he could stand with the beagle. She signaled two minutes. I shifted the puppy's leash to my other hand. My hands felt cold. Jeanne signaled one minute.

"And now a word from our friends at the Oakdale Dog Protection Society," said Roger.

Jeanne mouthed "You're on." I saw that the camera pointed right at my face had a red light. For a second I stared at it blankly in stark disbelief, then I said quickly, "I'm Brenna Matthews speaking for Oakdale's Dog Protection Society. I'd like you to meet some of our friends here who need good homes." I swallowed, regarding the camera as if it were a king cobra coming in for the kill. "This fellow is a bit of a

clown." Clown Dog regarded the camera lugu-
briously. "He's a happy-go-lucky little thing with
a real personality. He loves to play catch." I
looked dubiously at him, wishing I had been more
moderate in my praise when I had written the
script. He was showing all the personality and
energy of a dish cloth. Then suddenly, he sat up
and begged. "Look at that!" I squealed. "He's
begging for a home!" He grinned at the camera.
"What a ham!" Again I looked back at the
camera, mesmerized. Three minutes and two
dogs to go. I picked up the puppy quickly.

"Now here's a sweet puppy. We figure she's
about three months old. She loves to play, but
she'll need time to rest and grow, too. She looks
like she'll grow up to be a fairly large dog, so she
should have a home with a pretty good sized
yard." Figuring that puppies almost sell themselves, I moved quickly to the real challenge and
signalled Simon to bring on the beagle. "And now
here's another very special little dog. Beagles are
good hunting dogs and are very playful and
ingenious. See how alert he is? Look at the
intelligence in those eyes!" I had a momentary
qualm. Should I, in all honesty, have pointed out
that intelligence in dogs is not likely to be devoted
to higher education but to getting out of fenced
areas? I compromised with my conscience. "He
needs a strong-willed, active owner who will
enjoy out of door activities with him," I said. "If
you can give a home to any of these wonderful

dogs, we'd love to hear from you at the Dog
Protection Society. Call Oakdale 3-2460. That's
Oakdale 3-2460. Or call the Oakdale Police Station to get our number. We ask for a fifteen dollar
donation for each dog adopted to help cover
expenses. Remember our number, Oakdale
3-2460. Come see us and take a friend home with
you!"

The red light of the camera switched off, but I
still sat stiffly staring at the camera. I felt numb. It
was hard to believe my ordeal was really over.

Jeanne led Simon and me and the dogs out of
the studio and deposited us in the dark hall
outside. Through the glass window of the door, I
could see that Roger the Rodeo Clown was again
sitting on his stool gesturing enthusiastically while
Jeanne stood beside a camera, hugging her clip-
board, and regarded him with boredom. It was
over. I was finished. I steadied myself against the
wall. "How did I do?" I asked timidly.

"Great," said Simon, shifting his hold on the
leashes, "but next time blink."

"What?"

"Blink. You didn't blink the whole time."

I found that hard to believe. I blinked a few
times experimentally. The blinking apparatus was
still in order. "I guess I was concentrating on the
camera so hard," I said.

"You were great, anyway," said Simon. "And
what about that silly clown dog!"

"That really was a piece of luck. I had no idea

he could do that." I began walking in the direction of the red light of the exit. I was eager to put distance between me and the television cameras.

"What dogs do you think we should use next week?" asked Simon.

I nearly tripped on the leashes. Next week? Next week? What a ghastly thought!

7

When we got back to my house, Simon and I walked the dogs around back to the yard. I closed the gate behind me with a sense of relief. Simon and I went in the back door. In the family room, Jack, who was holding the phone to his ear with one shoulder, grimaced and made mute gestures of despair. He was giving the caller our address. He hung up with a bang. I had expected a ticker tape parade to celebrate my success, but I was beginning to suspect it wasn't going to work out that way. "Thank goodness you're home," said Jack. "You sure took your sweet time." Since we had come straight home without even stopping for a hamburger, this was unfair, but Jack seemed to be coming a bit unglued. "The phone is ringing off the hook," he said. "Mom and Dad are hiding out upstairs. Look, these guys will be here any minute. I'm going to need some help." The phone rang again, stridently. At the same time I heard the soft gong of the doorbell. I couldn't blame Mom and Dad for cowering upstairs. It was a bit overpowering.

The beagle turned out to be the first to ride off with his new family. He grinned out the window at us as they drove away. They had come all the way from Raleigh for the privilege of applying for ownership. I fervently hoped they knew what they were getting into.

"You did a great selling job on that one, Bren," said Simon.

"I guess I must have," I said, amazed.

The puppy went to a family with small children. They had seemed like very quiet, shy children when I showed them around to the backyard, but they let out squeals of delight when they saw the puppy. They sat down on the grass and let him hop all over them, licking their faces. "No, Nonny," the mother said firmly. "We do not pick doggies up by the ears." I was favorably impressed.

Clown Dog was adopted by an Oakdale trial lawyer who said that with the business he was in he could use a few laughs.

Unfortunately, the phone did not magically

stop ringing once all three dogs were adopted. It rang all afternoon. We learned there was no point in getting far from it, so we all sprawled in chairs in a semicircle around the phone in the family room and answered it in rotation.

"We ought to think of a way to harness this interest," I said. "It's the same principle as getting the homes to board the dogs in. You find a little bit of interest, you grab it and build on it. People say they want to help so you try to get them to board a dog or something. If they're willing to board a dog, you try to get them to agree to do it regularly. You build on what you have. Now we've got people interested in the dogs that they saw; we've got to build on that interest."

"We tell them we have other dogs," said Jack.

"I know," I said, my eyes narrowing as I planned. "But what we need is a central registry here at the house. In it will be a card on every dog we're taking care of together with its photograph. That way when people come out here and find out that the dog they had in mind is already adopted, we can give them an idea of everything we have."

"You may have something there," said Simon. "But it's too bad we can't keep the dogs in one location. There's no substitute for the person's actually seeing and playing with them."

After a while I began rooting around in the kitchen for something for us to eat. Simon and I had never had lunch. With ham sandwiches and dill pickles before us, we all began to feel more expansive.

"You really did a great job on the television, Bren," said Jack, biting deeply into his sandwich.

"Uhm," said Simon, a sound intended to indicate agreement while chewing, I gathered.

Mom and Dad at last ventured downstairs. Dad rumpled my hair. "You did a great job, sweetheart. We're proud of you."

"Couldn't have been better," crowed Mom.

At last, here it was, my ticker tape parade. The phone was continuing to ring but at wider intervals, so that conversation was now possible.

"I was going to ask you to stay to dinner, Simon," said Mom, "but you three look like you won't be hungry for quite a while yet."

"Thank you, Mrs. Matthews," said Simon. "But I need to be getting home."

What do you mean, getting home? I thought. This is supposed to be my parade, my celebration. Why do you have to be getting home now?

Jack and I walked with Simon out to his car. "Why don't you come back after supper and we'll finish our game," said Jack. His and Simon's chess game from Wednesday was still sitting on the coffee table.

"Can't tonight," said Simon. "What about tomorrow night?"

"Naah," said Jack. "I've got a date. Have I ever told you about Cindy Norton?" He leaned against the car door, then shot me a look that said get lost. There was no reason I should get lost so Jack could confide his dearest hopes and dreams about Cindy Norton to Simon, no reason except that if I didn't I would end up shouting "You can't make me" and "Nyah-nyah-nyah." I thought it wiser to retreat with my dignity intact.

I did not, however, speak to him when he returned.

"Why don't you kids go out and have a good time," said Dad. "Your mother and I can man the phone. We were going to go to the Civic Theater tonight but you can take our tickets and we'll have a quiet evening at home instead."

The ring of the phone punctuated his statement, casting some doubt on how quiet it would be.

"Gee," said Jack, "it would be great to get away from the phone, wouldn't it, Brenna?"

I said nothing as I was still pouting but, of course, Jack didn't notice.

"What time does it start?" Jack asked. "Will we have time to eat first?"

"It doesn't start until eight-thirty," said Mom.

I decided to quit sulking as unfortunately mine is a family in which you can sulk for many hours before someone notices.

After dinner, I put on my prettiest dress, the one that makes me look as if I have quite a respectable amount of bosom. After I dressed I twirled around and watched the skirt flare out, thinking that I really have quite nice legs. It was too bad of Simon to go tearing off at my moment of triumph, but no doubt he had to do something for his mother. I paused a moment, sympathizing with his mother working so hard and going to school, before I picked up my mascara wand. It was *sweet* of Simon to want to spend time with his mother. I slipped into my nicest pair of shoes, the delicate strappy ones that make my legs look even better and are perfect in every way except for walking or standing. After all, I reflected, apropos of Simon, where there is life there is hope. Perhaps every day that Simon got to know me better I was growing in his good opinion and one day soon he would look deep into my eyes and. . . .

"Brenna," Jack yelled, "are you going to take all night? We've got to go."

Mom and Dad were reading in the family room with their shoes off and their feet up.

"You look beautiful, sweetheart," said Dad as we went by, "perfectly beautiful."

"And don't worry about the telephone," said Mom. "We'll get along just fine."

Just then the telephone rang again and Jack and I beat a hasty retreat.

The parking lot was well filled when we arrived. We knew we were late so we hurried across the little bridge, startling the goldfish, and made our way past the willows and the stone lantern to the theater. Someday I planned to get to the theater early and sit admiring the goldfish, while others dashed frantically about. But tonight, as usual, we charged up the steps and had just slid breathlessly into our seats when the house lights went off. That's why I didn't see that Simon was there.

At intermission the lobby was crammed full of

people hoping in vain to have a turn at the restroom or the water fountain. Simon and Margarita practically ran right into us. Simon looked momentarily startled, then smiled at us. "You remember Jack and Brenna, don't you Margarita?" he said.

"I do," said Margarita, gracefully sidestepping a purposeful matron making her way through the crowd. "I love the work of Garcia Lorca," she said. "So poetic."

"Right," said Jack, no doubt momentarily stunned by the force of her perfume.

Diamante earrings glittered against her dark hair and her shoes were even higher-heeled and strappier than mine. They must have been sheer torture. She smiled and I saw that her lips were moist like those of models on lipstick commercials.

"Well, we'd better get moving," said Simon. "Margarita wants to see the garden before intermission is over."

"Of course," I murmured. They disappeared into the crush and Jack and I made our way back to our seats. I was amazed that acquaintances greeted me quite cheerfully as we passed. I felt such a searing pain in my midriff I felt sure I must have the white, drawn look of a patient with acute appendicitis, but no one seemed to notice.

Jack knew, however. That was almost the worst part, that Jack knew exactly how I felt. We went back to our seats without saying a word. I opened my program and looked at it with unseeing eyes.

"She's very pretty isn't she," I said finally.

"If you go for that type," said Jack, in tones of heavy disdain.

"Simon seems to," I said in a small voice.

It seemed like an extraordinarily long intermission, lots of time to imagine what Simon and Margarita must be doing in the Japanese garden. Of course, quite possibly a dispassionate interest in horticulture had propelled them there, but having seen Margarita's shoes, I knew she would have to have a very compelling motive to propose a walk.

Blood Wedding is a tragedy about frustrated women; it was not what I needed to see that night. In the car, afterwards, tears began to trickle down my cheeks. "Depressing story," I said.

"Yep," said Jack.

I began to hiccup.

8

The next morning I let the family go to church without me. "I feel a little sick," I said to Mom.

"All the excitement of that television spot has worn you out," she said sympathetically.

So, standing at the kitchen window in my bathrobe, I watched Dad and Jack fold their long frames into the car. Then the red poppies on Mom's straw hat bobbed a little as she got in, and they drove off. I was alone in the house listening to the hum of the refrigerator. Almost at once the phone rang—someone inquiring about the puppy. I suppose there are always a few deliberate souls who like to sleep on any decision. But as it turned out there were only a few phone calls all morning and I was able to fully concentrate on feeling perfectly rotten. I would go to the window, look out in the backyard at Guest Dog luxuriating in the sunshine and sigh, "Poor Guest Dog. He's all alone now." Then I would wipe a trickling tear off my nose and sit down again to listen to the hum of the refrigerator.

After church, Dad went back to the office to catch up on some work, Mom busied herself with paint remover on the driveway, and Jack, to the fascination of Guest Dog, was working out with weights in the backyard. Everyone was busy and happy except me. I was feeling rotten. I almost jumped up and went over to cry on Janey's shoulder, but I decided against it. Janey, who was developing a deep tan from all those hours on the sailboat, showed a distressing tendency to chirrup on for hours about Gary. In my weakened state, I was sure I wasn't up to facing a chirrup.

The chief challenge of the day was dinner. That night, when we all sat down at the table, I discovered that tears could begin to well up in my eyes with no greater provocation than my asking for the salt and pepper. I knew I was going to have to make an extra effort to appear that all was well.

"Is Jack gone again?" asked Daddy irritably. "I make an effort to be home for dinner. You would think he could, too."

"He's taking Cindy Norton out to dinner," Mom explained.

"How is he ever going to save any money if he keeps taking people out to dinner?" grumbled Dad.

Now was the time for me to tell some amusing little anecdote to show how light-of-heart I was. The problem was that in my present state nothing struck me as amusing. I decided to settle for cheerful. "Beautiful weather we're having, isn't it?" I said.

"Are you out of your mind?" said Dad, glaring at me incredulously. "It must be a hundred degrees in the shade out there!"

Tears began to well up in my eyes again.

"Pay no attention to him, Brenna," said Mom. "Your father has had a bad day."

He has had a bad day! What about me? After dinner, when I carried my dishes to the kitchen, I could hear Mother saying, "It's not our fault your dictaphone is broken, George. You could at least try to be civil at the dinner table."

The next morning, Jack announced that Simon would be coming over after supper. I was pleased to have warning of it. After my lousy performance at the dinner table the night before, I knew my acting ability wouldn't measure up to the challenge of pretending everything was all right in front of Simon. I packed up a notebook and pencil and prepared to head for the library before he appeared.

"I'm going to do some research on veterinary science as a career," I told Mom. She beamed. It must have seemed to her as if suddenly I had as much direction as one of the points of the compass. Little did she know my heart was breaking and my life was ashes.

The library is one part of Oakdale which has not been touched by the city fathers' passion for renovation. I suppose nothing whatever has touched the library in the past sixty years or so except an odd dust cloth. The entrance is planted with red geraniums. Three big trees, heavy with their summer leaves, frame the building. As you go in the entry hall, there's a display case with Indian arrowheads, some fossil bones, and a small octopus pickled in formaldehyde. Against the other wall is a life-sized Greek statue of a boy picking a thorn out of his foot. Honor having been done in this manner to both art and science, the effort at decoration evidently collapsed. The rest of the library is furnished simply with big oak tables, chairs, and somber portraits of former library board members. Mrs. Odum at the circulation desk whispered hello as I passed. I went to the Careers shelf, pulled out *So You Want to Be a Veterinarian,* and sat down with it at one of the library's tremendously heavy, long oak tables. If the winds of change ever do sweep through Oakdale Memorial Library, they're going to have a heck of a time moving those tables out.

I turned to page one and stared sightlessly at it. Now that I considered it dispassionately I could see that Simon and Margarita were a natural pair—like bookends. They both had that dark, vivid look and that ineffable not-from-Oakdale quality. It all seemed very neat and logical. I felt terrible. I looked around me despairingly. Considering it was summer and there were no research papers to write, the library was surprisingly full of people. Maybe they were all people looking forward to two weeks at the beach who decided they would spend that time lying on the beach reading *War and Peace*.

Tom Parsons was standing at the New Books shelf. He caught sight of me and smiled in my direction. It was too late to lose myself in my book, so I managed to smile back. He pulled a shiny, bright-colored book off the shelf and came over to my table. I saw that he had *How to Restore Your Vintage MG*.

"Having a good summer?" he asked.

"Great," I said wanly.

"Won't be too long 'til school starts."

"No," I agreed.

"Just about a month, I figure. Boy, the time sure does fly when you're having a good time."

"Uh-huh."

"Well, see you around." He beat an escape.

I hoped Tom hadn't been looking for sparkling conversation. I propped my chin in my hand. The advantage of this was that it was one way to hold my head up. I noticed that the stiff leaves of an oak branch were brushing against the round, leaded window in the corner near me. It was surprising I had never before noticed how sinister the shadowy corners of the library were, how bleak the florescent lighting was, how deeply depressing it all was. I wondered how long Simon would stay at the house. To be on the safe side, I decided I'd better stay until the library closed at nine.

I determinedly settled down to my book. Unfortunately, it only had fifty pages. After I finished I could have read the whole thing again because I certainly didn't grasp much of it the first time around, but I began to worry that someone would notice I was reading it again and again. In the end I was reduced to reading about the life cycle of the liver fluke in *National Geographic*. Finally at five of nine the lights blinked their warning signal. There was a general migration to the circulation desk, and I left.

It was always dark inside the library because of its narrow old-fashioned windows, but now it was growing dark outside, too, and the flowers of the geraniums had darkened from crimson to carmine in the dusk. There would be other men in my life, I told myself. Consider how Tom Parsons had come over to say hello. The thought didn't cheer me up a bit.

I began to get a panicky feeling as I got close to home. What if Simon was still there? I decided that if his car was still out front I would just keep driving and take refuge at Janey's house. But when I got to the house his car wasn't there. For an awful moment it occurred to me that maybe he hadn't come at all. Maybe he couldn't make it and was going to come tomorrow night instead. Could I stand another evening with the liver fluke?

"Simon asked where you were," Jack said as I walked in the kitchen. I didn't know what to say to that so I opened the refrigerator. I could see it now—*My Life as a Fugitive* by Brenna Matthews. The moving story of a young girl's fight to avoid seeing a boy named Simon.

Mom and Dad were engrossed in a television program so I didn't have to face any searching questions about veterinary science as a career. I took a Coke to my room to brood in peace.

My only hope, I decided, was to throw myself into my work. If the dull ache in my midriff never subsided, at least I would be able to point to a worthwhile life spent in the service of the dogs of Oakdale. The next morning I brought two dogs from the outlying farms in to my house, which I thought of as the central adoption agency. I also made a neat, tasteful wooden sign for our mailbox saying "Dog Protection Society," to make it easier for people to find the house. I borrowed Dad's Polaroid to make a portrait gallery of all our charges for a central file at my house.

We got several calls during the week and two people came by the house to look at the dogs. I thought that was a good sign. It showed that people thought of us as a permanent source of dogs, that we didn't fly out of their minds as soon as the television spot was over.

Wednesday a very old lady came by. She wore a little felt hat with artificial violets on it, and her white hair was arranged in ringlets under a hair net. The polite young man in a peaked cap who was driving her helped her out of the car and guided her up the steps. I was relieved to see she hadn't driven herself. I can't help but feel that people who have to be guided to the front door don't have the reflexes for today's traffic.

This old lady wasn't like most of the old ladies I know, who wear polyester pants suits and pump their own gas. She reminded me more of my great-grandmother, who died when I was ten. She wore the same little black lace-up shoes, and I noticed with fascination that, like my great-grandmother, she had fastened the draped neck-line of her dress with a pearl pin. Her dress had that sort of squiggly circle and dot design that looks like a purple pen and ink drawing of fried eggs. "Good morning, young lady," she said. "I am interested in getting a dog."

I realized I had been staring and brought myself up short. "Uh, of course," I said. "Come right in. We only have a few dogs right here at the house, but we have a number of others that are boarded out to people who live on farms. If you'd like to look through our files you can see what is available."

"I'd like to see what you have here," she said,

taking some gold-rimmed glasses out of her purse and putting them on, the better to see.

The problem with this was that what we had on hand was Guest Dog, an extremely rowdy Labrador retriever, and a mutt that looked like a sled dog and had the disposition of a wolf.

I took her around to the back fence while I thought fast. I was afraid to even let her in the gate, much less adopt one of these monsters. I was going to have to think how to tactfully suggest to her that this sort of dog wasn't suitable for her.

Guest Dog and the Lab saw us and came running over, falling over each other in their eagerness. Guest Dog put his paws on the gate and licked my face wetly while the Lab ran in circles. The sled dog grinned at us wolfishly from the distance.

"Have you ever considered a cat?" I said baldly. This was not quite the tactful approach I had planned, so I hastily went on. "The thing is that we get a lot of large, active dogs. The average toy dog doesn't often come up for adoption. Now you take the Lab . . ." The Lab, after running around in loose-jointed, lolloping strides, had come to rest at the gate and was standing before us panting. "It's a great dog," I said, "for a big person who spends a lot of time out of doors, somebody who has a strong personality and wouldn't have any trouble controlling her." I perceived a dangerous glint in the old lady's eye that indicated that though frail she was a strong

personality herself, and went on desperately,
"You see a dog like that is a working dog. You
have to give her tasks, teach her to retrieve, let
her swim, fetch, race. If she isn't kept busy, she'll
be into mischief all the time. These big dogs are
all a lot of work. The sheep dog needs brushing
every day." I didn't feel it was necessary to warn
her against the sled dog whose wolfish grin and
aloof manner were unlikely to appeal to the
casual visitor.

"You don't seem to be very anxious to get rid of
these dogs, young lady," she said crisply.

"We do want to find them permanent homes,"
I said, "but it's important that they *fit* the homes.
I don't think so many dogs would be abandoned if
people knew what they were getting into before
they ever got the dog to begin with. Now a cat is
naturally gentle and undemanding. They don't
need walking, rarely need brushing, eat very
little . . ."

She turned away from the fence decisively.
"Perhaps you are right," she said. "I will look
into getting a cat." I breathed a silent sigh of
relief as we walked together towards her car. The
young man who had been leaning on the mud
guard straightened up respectfully as we appeared.

"You have quite an impressive organization
here," she said.

Still luxuriating in the relief of having dissuaded
her from adopting the Lab, I spoke cheerfully.

"Thank you. We've really gotten organized. I think now that we have the TV spot, we can place three or four dogs a week. We're working under some disadvantages, but I think we're doing okay."

As I watched them drive away, I noticed that the radiator cap had a pretty silver ornament. I like those sleek long-hooded cars. You don't see very many of them.

The family that came that afternoon was much more suited to adopt a dog. I could tell it the minute they piled noisily out of their station wagon. I was particularly pleased to see a husky twelve-year-old boy climb out of the back seat. A twelve year old can give a big dog quite a work-out. The mother explained to me that now that they had moved into a house with a fenced backyard, they had decided to get a dog. What did I have? The three children streamed into the backyard and, to my dismay, immediately fixed on Guest Dog as the object of their affections. I was surprised to find myself explaining to the mother, "The sheep dog isn't up for adoption, just the other two. I do have a file on some others you might be interested in. We have a very nice sheep dog type boarding at a farm near here."

"Oh, I think I like the Lab," she said, reaching over the fence to pet him. "I used to have a Lab when I was little. Come over here, kids. Isn't she sweet?"

I considered the matter clinched. Already I had learned that "I had one when I was little" meant you could consider the dog adopted. And sure enough within a half hour the Lab was piling into the station wagon with them, the regulation fifteen dollars having changed hands, and instructions on care and feeding having been duly given.

I picked up the brush and ruefully began to groom Guest Dog, whom I had so suddenly realized I couldn't give up. "I couldn't let them take one of the founding members of the Dog Protection Society, could I?" I said. He smiled at me. "I guess if you're mine now I'll have to give you a name, won't I?" I put the brush down and regarded him contemplatively. "Now what do you remind me of?" His eyes, indolently half closed, regarded me with amiable arrogance and suddenly I was reminded of Simon. I began brushing him fiercely.

The phone began ringing distantly inside the house. I jumped up suddenly and ran in to get it, banging my shin on a kitchen chair as I made the final leap for it. It was Janey.

"What's the matter. You sound awful," she said.

I clenched my teeth. "Nothing. I just banged myself on the kitchen chair."

"Oh. Well, you know how you said you'd stop by tomorrow to bring the dog food? I wonder if you could do it today instead. Gary wants me to go sailing with him tomorrow."

"Sure. I'll come over as soon as I finish brushing Guest Dog."

"Are you sure you're okay? You sure sound funny."

I tried to unclench my teeth. "I'm fine. I'll be there soon," I said shortly. I would just have to brace myself for Janey's ecstasies on true love.

I took the camera with me to Janey's. I needed a snapshot of her ugly duckling dog for my central file. While Janey carried the dog food into the kitchen, I posed the critter by the picket fence and tried to make him smile.

"What are you doing?" asked Janey, coming out the kitchen door.

"I'm getting a picture for my central file," I said. "I'm thinking seriously of letting him be one of the three we put on this week's television spot, too. That television thing is amazing. We had every one of the three dogs we showed last week adopted in a matter of hours."

"What's the rush?"

"What do you mean, what's the rush? You're the one who told me you were going on vacation."

She looked uncomfortable. "Well, I'm not sure I want him to be adopted."

I tried not to look indecently jubilant. I had had my doubts that even television could move this one.

I said, in what I hoped was a businesslike way, "Members of the society are exempted from paying the fifteen dollar adoption fee. Consider him yours."

Janey sat down on the back stoop. "This is so sudden," she said. "Maybe I'd better think about it for a while."

"What's to think about? How is Gary getting along?" I asked, deftly changing the subject.

As I had thought, Janey's second thoughts slipped away like melting jello and she launched into a glowing account of her relationship with Gary. "There's never been a boy I felt so close to," she said. "With Gary I am completely at ease."

I had been completely at ease with Gary, too. My only problem was a tendency to fall asleep in his presence.

"Didn't I see you uptown last week with a good-looking guy?" she asked me. Clearly she was willing to give me equal time to talk about my love life. Unfortunately, I didn't want equal time.

"Well," I said, "you know Jack, Dad, and Sergeant Mulhoney, so if it wasn't them, it must have been Simon."

"Dark hair, blue eyes, carrying a bag of dog food?"

"That's Simon."

"Who's Simon? Is he the new love interest in your life?"

"Actually, he's a friend of Jack's." I made a valiant attempt to sound as if I were making normal civilized conversation. "He's been a terrific help with the dogs. It was his idea to do the television spot. He set it up."

"What's he like?"

"I thought Gary filled your whole life," I said coldly.

"What's the matter with you?" asked Janey. "You certainly are being disagreeable. Just because I'm going with Gary does not mean I've totally lost interest in the world around me. I just asked what he was like."

"I'm sorry," I said, sitting down on the back stoop. "Well, he is . . . very nice. I mean, you know, willing to help out. Likes dogs." I didn't feel that this sketch told at all what Simon was like, but if I started getting into that, I would soon have been pouring my broken heart out all over the back stoop, and it was already grim enough at home, with Jack being tactful, a spectacle which in happier times would have been funny.

"He doesn't look like a guy from Oakdale, somehow," said Janey. "It's hard to put your finger on. Maybe it's his clothes."

While it is true that Simon's clothes were occasionally of a different color or brand than was currently available at Oakdale's three men's stores, they were certainly in no way exotic. I refrained from comment, however, lest I burst out that yes, he was different, very different from the other guys and altogether better, an observation that seemed certain to arouse suspicion.

"Maybe it's not his clothes," said Janey.

"Maybe it's something about the way he moves. Would you say he's conceited?"

"I would not," I said. Actually, I would have said exactly that a couple of months ago, but I just didn't think of him that way anymore.

"He's just an ordinary nice guy," I said firmly. "And he's not just a friend of Jack's really. He's a friend of mine, too."

Janey looked out distantly at the field behind her yard and a little smile played on her lips. "It's a shame to waste a guy like that on friendship," she said.

I refused to be drawn in. "I'd better shove along on home," I said. "I need to practice blinking. I've got that television spot on Saturday." I did a few practice blinks.

"I'm sorry I missed you on it last Saturday," said Janey, "but Gary and I . . ."

"Were out sailing," I finished for her. "That's okay. Don't worry about it. It's not exactly the dramatic presentation of the century. I just show the dogs and try to keep from passing out from fright."

"It'll get easier as you go on," said Janey reassuringly. "You'll probably get to be very blasé about being on television."

I considered this possibility a moment and rejected it as too bizzare to seriously consider. "I don't think so," I said.

"This time, I'm determined to see it," said Janey. "Gary and I will be sitting here on Saturday with eyes glued to the set at twelve o'clock sharp."

I brightened. Since I was on at eleven-thirty, it seemed likely they would miss me. "Right," I said. "Maybe after you hear my spiel you'll decide to adopt another dog."

"Ha!" said Janey.

It occurred to me as I drove off that this business of the boarders adopting dogs was not a practice we wanted to encourage. It was easier to get new dog owners, who were drawn from the entire population, than it was to get new boarders, who were made up only of people we knew who had farms or big fenced yards. Already I had adopted Guest Dog and reduced the boarding capacity of my backyard by one third, and Janey had adopted the ugly duckling dog, further reducing our boarding capacity. I figured we were getting about one to two new strays a week. If we successfully found homes for three a week, we could stay ahead of ourselves, but if we began losing boarding capacity, we could end up in trouble again. Sometimes the responsibility of it all wore me down.

Today as I drove home from Janey's there were no pleasant visions, just the trees lining the street. They looked unpleasantly solid. You thought about how their roots were down deep holding onto clay and gravel and how you'd have the devil of a time digging one up if you should decide you'd rather have tulips instead. It made me think about the unbudgeable quality reality has. Like it or not, there it is. And Simon and Margarita were definitely there.

All I could hope was that maybe eventually I would get resigned to the whole thing, like those wise men who live in loincloths in caves in the Himalayas and are above it all.

9

The next day something happened that, had it not been for my sweet and forgiving nature, would have meant the end of a beautiful friendship. The day began peacefully enough with my dragging out the old washtub and dip. I didn't dare go over and use Simon's fine new dipping pit for fear of running into him, so it was back to the dark ages with the washtub and brute force. Happily the wolf dog proved fairly amenable to the dipping, as was the new addition to my backyard kennel, a fuzzy brown dog. The former owner of the brown dog, an engineer who had been suddenly transferred to England, had informed me that it was a cocker-poodle and Pekinese mix, making it a cocka-peke-apoo.

The dipping taken care of, I returned to the house for my next task, washing my candlewicktype bedspread. Since the thing weighed a ton and took about a day and a half to dry in the drier, I could only face washing it about twice a year. Already it had thrown the washing machine out of balance twice with its immense weight, but at last it was washed and I was bracing myself to haul it out of the machine and stuff it into the drier for its long sojourn there. It was just at this point that Janey peeked in the door.

"Just thought I'd drop by and say hello," she said. "Should I have called first? I just finished at the day care and do I ever need a break!"

"Come on in. You missed dipping the dogs but you're just in time to help me get this thing in the drier. It weighs a ton when it's wet." Janey readily came over to help me with the thing. It had anchored itself to the agitator and almost seemed to take on life as it resisted our efforts to get it out of the washer, wrapping itself around our arms and flopping over on our heads in a manner reminiscent of the more gory depictions of the sea serpents strangling Laocoön.

"What a monster!" Janey exclaimed when at length we had the thing heaped in a clothes basket which was buckling under its weight. "You mean you sleep under that thing? Doesn't it squash your toes?"

"It's not this heavy when it's dry," I said. "The only thing is it takes forever to get dry."

"You should hang it up outside," said Janey. "It'll save on electricity. All that hot summer sun is free."

I thought about that a minute and it seemed like a good idea. I figured the clothesline could take the weight if I was careful to distribute it over two of the lines so they would share the weight.

"Maybe you're right," I said. "I'll hang it up outside."

"Sure I'm right," said Janey. "Wait a minute. I've got something out in the car I want to show you. You remember that layette I've been embroidering for my brother's new baby? I've finally finished. I'm going to go get it. Can you manage that bedspread all right?"

"Sure," I said. "Just let me get my pack elephant."

But Janey was already halfway out the door to go to her car. I didn't try to lift the laundry basket. I just kicked it along the kitchen floor. Once out at the clothesline, I lifted first one corner of the thing then another, taking care to use three clothespins at each juncture. I judged that the clothesline would hold it. At least as yet there were no signs of imminent collapse. The dogs regarded me with interest as I erected a huge wall of wet white bedspread in the backyard. "Now don't you get any ideas about pawing at this," I said sternly. They looked at me with open-eyed innocence. Then I heard Janey coming around back. She had decided to bring the layette around to the backyard to show me. The dogs took up the alarm as she reached the gate, her arms full of a large, flat box from which tufts of tissue paper peeked out. "Help! Burglars! Thieves!" the three dogs barked.

"Hush," I said severely. "It's only Janey."

Janey balanced the box on one hand and opened the gate with the other, kicking it more fully open with her heel so she could pass. "Wait till you see these," she bubbled. "It's taken me months, but it's worth it. They're going to be heirlooms."

"Janey, the gate!" I shrieked, spilling all the clothespins. "Close the gate, for Pete's sake."

Janey looked around her, bewildered, as suddenly all three dogs streaked past her feet and out the gate.

"You let them out!" I screamed. "I can't believe this. How are we ever going to get them back?" I took off running.

"Don't they come when you call?" I heard Janey ask blankly as I skidded past her. I didn't have the time to give her a withering glance—the dogs were ahead of me. I wouldn't have thought Guest Dog had it in him to move so fast. Janey put the layette down and followed me. Out front the dogs were running in a pack, celebrating their adventure by nipping at each other's heels and playing leap frog.

"Come back here," I yelled.

"They don't seem to be paying attention," Janey said nervously. The dogs were frolicking down the street running in crazy circles.

The next door neighbor came out to see what the commotion was about. Two houses down, Mrs. Giles, a widow who devotes her life to keeping her yard free of weeds, peeked out the window. Recently, Mrs. Giles had decided she was not making satisfactory progress in her battle against weeds. Not contented to have the best lawn in the neighborhood, she had plowed up and reseeded the entire front yard, aiming to have the best lawn in Oakdale.

"Look, I'm going in the house to get some cookies to use as bait," I told Janey. Running in, I rooted around desperately in the refrigerator and came up with a lamb bone, a hunk of cheese, and, from the cookie jar, three chocolate chip cookies. When I came out bearing all these inducements, I saw a sight that froze my blood. The dogs, still tripping the light fantastic up and down our street, were headed straight for Mrs. Giles newly reseeded lawn.

"Stop!" I shrieked. "Come back here!" Mrs. Giles, standing at her window, had covered her face with her hands, unable to watch the coming disaster. I ran with all my might, but the dogs beat me there and landed square in the nicely raked and sifted topsoil of her front yard. Guest Dog rolled over and burrowed down in the nice smelling earth. The cocka-peke-apoo started digging a hole. I stood on the sidewalk and held out all my goodies.

"Want a nice cookie?" I wheedled. "Nice lamb bone? Nicems cheese?"

Guest Dog lifted his nose to sniff the air. Hmm. Aged cheese. Perhaps he would take a bite. He took a few careless digs at the ground and then began to amble over towards me.

"Janey," I said, my teeth clenched, "come help me. Grab his collar."

While he was concentrating on the cheese, Janey grabbed him. He didn't drag her twenty feet along the sidewalk as I had half expected and even hoped, but stood peacefully beside her. The cookies lured the other two dogs. Within minutes I had them both by their collars and we were frog marching them back to the backyard. I pushed them in, slammed the gate, and leaned against it. "At last," I said.

Suddenly a strange expression played across Janey's face. "Eeek!" she exclaimed. "Yuck! Oh, no!" I wheeled around and saw Guest Dog rolling over and over on my white candlewick bedspread, which was sagging disasterously from the clothesline. The finely sifted dirt of Mrs. Giles' yard, which of late had been clinging to his coat, was now turning to mud on my bedspread. I covered my eyes, but not before I saw him place one black paw square on the bedspread and give himself a royal shake.

I collected myself enough to scream incoherently, "Get away from there you wretched dog! Bad, bad dog!" I squeezed through the gate, taking care to close it securely behind me, and ran to the bedspread. It looked as if the whole track team had wiped its feet on it. I gathered up its muddy expanse, groaning, and dumped it into the clothes basket. As I dragged the heavily laden basket towards the house to begin the laundering all over again, I saw that Janey was picking up her layette box, which in all the excitement had been left at the gate. She hugged it to her protectively. "Thank goodness they didn't get to the baby clothes," she said. I made no comment but kicked the clothes basket through the back door.

After I again stuffed the big bedspread into the washing machine, I began to feel more calm. After all, I thought philosophically, there are bound to be ups and downs when you deal with as many dogs as I do every week, in one way or another. When Janey presented the layette for my inspection, I even dutifully admired it.

She closed the box up. "I'm going to get this in the mail this afternoon," she said, "and this weekend I'm not going to so much as look at an embroidery hoop." She sighed with satisfaction. "Are you doing anything special this weekend?" she asked.

"Why, yes," I said with a trace of asperity, "I expect I'm going to be reseeding Mrs. Giles' lawn."

That was just one example of how the dogs managed to fill up my life. They may not have made it fun, but they certainly filled it up.

The following day I took three dogs in for parvo virus vaccines. "Is it hard to get into vet school?" I asked Dr. Briggs.

"Some people say it's harder to get into than medical school," he said. "There are fewer schools, you see."

I wondered idly if I could get into vet school. My grades would really need to be top notch, particularly in math and science, but now that I was living for work, my grades, which were already good, should begin to glimmer like platinum.

I imagined myself taking out a bank loan to build a small but modern animal hospital, working night and day, sitting up with feverish Pekineses. Well, why not? Then when my loveless life drew to a close and the question was asked did this woman have any redeeming social value, the answer would be yes.

But for now I had to cope as best I could. One thing I had to deal with was that there was no way of getting out of Simon's taking me to the TV station on Saturday. There was no help for it. I would just have to do the best I could to act normal.

So when Saturday morning came I had two things to dread—the acting in front of the television camera and the acting in the car on the way there. When Simon showed up at the house, I was struck again with how surprisingly hard it is to act normal if you concentrate on it. It's like blinking on television, the easiest thing in the world if you don't have to think about it, but once you start thinking about it you can't remember quite how it's done. Feeling like a marionette, I got into the car. Clearly I could have no future as a spy. The authorities would only have to look at my sitting there like a mannequin, to know I had something to conceal. "You, young lady," they would shout, "hand over those top secret documents!"

"Brenna," Simon said.

I started.

He looked at me with concern. "Look, if this television thing is really getting to you, maybe we ought to see if Jack can do it."

I felt all teary. Dear Simon, so thoughtful, so considerate. "I'll be okay," I choked.

"Let's sing "Old MacDonald," he said. "That will take your mind off it." We turned onto the open highway.

I felt pretty silly at first singing "Old MacDonald had a farm," but I had to say it took my mind off my troubles. It takes a lot of concentration to get all those "oink oink oinks" and "moo moo moos" in the right order. I began to giggle.

"You're looking better already," said Simon. I did feel better. Probably singing would turn out to have some hidden medicinal effect like those flowers that the old mountain people have always used that turned out to be full of aspirin.

"My family always used to sing on long trips,"

said Simon, "so I know all those songs with fifteen verses."

"Like 'Alouette,'" I said.

"And 'Ninety-nine Bottles of Beer on the Wall.'"

"And 'Mrs. Murphy's Chowder,'" I said. I blinked and stretched my fingers in my old expert way. Wheee! Easy as pie. I could do this all day. So what if Simon was crazy about Margarita, I told myself resolutely. I'll get along somehow.

I told Simon about the various people who had come to look at dogs during the week. Then I told him about what Dr. Briggs had said about getting into vet school. Now that I had come unfrozen I was a veritable chatterbox.

"You think you might want to be a vet?" he said.

"I don't know. It's too soon to say for sure. But I want to be able to do it if I want. I can't go wrong working harder in school. You never hear somebody saying 'The one thing I regret is that I got such good grades.'"

"Oh, I don't know," said Simon. "I remember reading once about this guy who was valedictorian at Berkeley and when he got up to give his valedictory address at the graduation what he said was 'Ladies and gentlemen, it wasn't worth it.'"

From the tone, I deduced that all was not well in Simon's world. "Have you heard anything more about Santo Domingo?" I ventured.

"Lots," said Simon gloomily. "Dad wants me to bring my passport up to date."

"Oh, dear."

"Maybe I'll see the bright side once I get there," he said bitterly.

It struck me that he was probably sad about having to leave Margarita. General gloom fell on the car.

At the television station we were greeted like old friends by the lady with the smile. Since we didn't have the beagle to contend with, Simon didn't have to come into the studio with me this time but waited outside.

This week I felt different on camera than I had last week. Now I was more conscious of what was going on. Like when you learn to swim. You quit worrying about how to stay above water and start thinking about going someplace. I could feel the heat of the lights and my dry mouth, but mainly my thoughts were on the dogs. I knew I couldn't count on having another showman like Clown Dog. I had to make my own luck this week, so I had brought along a tiny squeaky toy that fit in the palm of my hand. When the camera zoomed in on the first dog, I gently squeaked the little toy. The dog pricked up his ears and cocked his head, wondering what in the world was going on with my hand. "Look at his sweet expression," I said. I had the theory that dogs, like people, are individuals and I had kept quizzing the people boarding the dogs until I found something I could say about each one as an individual. "This fella loves to swim," I said. "He actually sleeps with his chin in his water bowl! It would be nice if he could have a home of his own near a lake." I turned my attention to the cocka-peke-apoo. "Now this lively fluffy girl here," I squeaked my toy at her to make sure she would look lively, "loves children. She also loves to chase chickens, but if you don't keep chickens she should work out fine for you. You can tell by looking at her that she has a loving but independent spirit." The cocka-peke-apoo smiled confidingly at me.

The third dog, the wolf dog, bristled as the camera man shifted his position and began to bark. "A terrific watchdog!" I said, ad libbing desperately. I tightened my grip on his leash. A little fiestiness might be admirable, but it wouldn't do anything for this dog's future if he should dive for the camera man's ankle. The camera man backed away to a safer distance and the wolf dog settled down with a warning growl. "This type of dog is suspicious of strangers," I went on, "but a loyal friend." To my relief, the dog immediately sat down and looked noble, like a Roman emperor. It was really amazing the way the dogs came through, as if they knew they had to sell themselves.

At last Jeanne gave me the cut sign and the red light went off. By now I knew my way out of the studio. As I left, I noticed that there was a monitor in the room. You could theoretically catch glimpses of yourself now and then, between sincere smiles into the camera, and see how it was going if you wanted to. I wasn't at all sure I did.

"You're getting to be a real pro," said Simon,

meeting me at the door. "That was a nasty moment when the white one started to bark, but you managed it fine."

I was quiet going home. I thought about how once my big ambition was to have Simon see that I was a person. Now he treated me like a person and I was no happier. I wanted him to treat me like a girl. I imagined myself telling him how I felt. Perhaps just as they were saying "Flight 301 to Santo Domingo now boarding at gate six" I would blurt out, "Good-bye Simon. I adore you." The timing was crucial. The trick was to fix it so that he wouldn't have time to reply "But Brenna, I think of you as a friend." Or even worse, "My heart belongs to another." I shuddered.

Simon reached over and patted my knee. "Calm down, kiddo," he said. "It's all over."

"Until next week," I said.

His brow wrinkled. "Seriously, do you want me to lean on Jack to do it? I'd volunteer myself but . . ."

But he wouldn't be here.

"That's all right," I said bravely. "It wasn't bad at all this time. It won't be long before I'll be perfectly blasé about the whole thing."

"Brenna?" He darted a quick, uncomfortable glance at me.

"What?"

"Uh, do you know all the words to 'Mrs. Murphy's Chowder'?"

I didn't, but the rest of the way home Simon taught them to me.

Just like last Saturday, the phone was ringing itself silly as we stepped in the door at home. Mom and Dad had taken the precaution this week of taking in a movie matinee.

"They went to see *Bambi?*" I said incredulously.

Jack shrugged. "That's all that was playing." The phone again began its clamor and he jumped for it.

Perhaps we should get one of those phones that just blinks a light instead of ringing. There was no getting around that all this ringing was a bit nerve wracking. Still, by the end of the day we had got all three dogs adopted, which is what counted.

Even Wolf Dog, about whom I had had my doubts, was adopted by an elderly man living in the country. He was looking for a watchdog and had been most impressed by Wolf Dog's fierce performance. "I like a spirited dog," he said. I had to admit that he and the wolf dog seemed like a good match. Not that Mr. Abel was like a wolf. He was more the lamb type, with soft-looking white hair and a gentle voice. But unlike most prospective owners, who walk right over to a dog and rumple its fur, Mr. Abel sat down in a lawn chair. "I want to see if he'll come over to me," he explained. I had to leave to help answer the doorbell, but when I returned Mr. Abel had made progress. Wolf Dog had drawn close to him and seemed so interested that he forgot to automatically bare his teeth when I opened the gate. In a short time they were fast friends. The wolf dog wasn't really fierce, as Mr. Abel commented, just reserved and very alert. When they drove away together, I felt as I suppose managers of lonely hearts organizations feel when they are successful with a match.

The cocka-peke-apoo adoption was a good match, too. You know how people are always saying that owners resemble their dogs? I don't hold much with that theory. After all, if I resembled Guest Dog I would have to be a two-hundred pound platinum blond with a wet nose. But on rare occasions I have felt there was something to the theory. You wouldn't have thought it was possible for a person to look like a cocka-peke-apoo, but the minute I opened the door to this woman, I knew which dog she had come for.

"I don't know why," she explained, as she picked her way towards the backyard in tiny high-heeled shoes, "but the minute I saw that little dog I felt drawn to her." I felt I could have told her why but I tactfully remained silent. I don't think people are charmed when you tell them they have eyes like a cocker spaniel, hair like a poodle, and a nose like a Pekinese. "Hello, sweetsums!" she exclaimed. "You know, it's the oddest thing, but it's like she reminds me of someone. Isn't that silly?" She laughed merrily. I echoed her with an unconvincing chuckle. "I just know this dog and I are going to love each other," she said. I, for one, didn't doubt it.

All three dogs adopted, at six I pulled TV dinners out of the oven and we sat in a circle around the telephone to eat. Of course, for Simon and Jack a TV dinner is more like an hors d'oeuvre, so they also made stacks of salami sandwiches.

"You two sure seem down," said Jack, "I thought we did pretty well. Don't you think people seem more willing to take on dogs than they were last week?"

Simon stretched out his legs awkwardly under the TV tray. Then he said bluntly, "I'm supposed to start packing my bags for the Dominican Republic."

"No!" said Jack. "When are you leaving?" Jack looked really upset. I suppose Simon was the best friend he ever had. "Good grief," Jack went on, not waiting for Simon to answer. "How long will you have to stay? I can't believe he's doing this to you," he exclaimed. Compared to Jack, I came off looking like a stoic.

Simon looked more gloomy than ever as he contemplated his small portion of tater tots and the blueberry muffin with peas stuck in it. "He thinks it's the right thing for me to do," he said. "I don't know what I could have done," he said. "Nobody could have worked on the Spanish any harder than I have this summer."

Jack ran his fingers through his hair in despair. "My gosh, yes. And the *hours* you've spent with Margarita . . ."

I winced.

Simon went on in a cooler tone of voice. "I don't think he really thinks I'm goofing off," he said. "He's just really anxious for me to do better. He says he thinks I should spend my senior year in Santo Domingo."

"Good grief," wailed Jack. "Your senior year, yet. That's going to wrack up your college applications for sure."

"Dad doesn't think so," said Simon. "He says, after all, this is going to be my life after school. He doesn't want me to end up speaking pidgin Spanish."

"Pidgin Spanish!" Jack exclaimed unbelievingly. I knew from Jack that Simon's Spanish was the admiration of Mrs. Olefin, the Spanish teacher at the high school.

"And there's the culture," Simon went on steadily. "Dad thinks I should have a better feel for the Dominican way of life. He says he's rethinking the whole college thing and wondering if Madrid wouldn't be a better choice than an American school."

"Madrid!" keened Jack. "The man is loopy."

I shot Jack a warning glance. Our parents had drilled into us many times that it was one thing for people to criticize their own family and another thing for outsiders to. And come to think of it, you didn't hear Simon criticize his father, really.

"What does your mother think about it?" I asked tentatively.

"She says she's sure Dad only wants what's best for me. It's a funny thing with Mother. She really wants to have me around, so I think she's decided she has to be unselfish and let me go."

"Well, they can't tie you up and drag you to the plane," snorted Jack.

Simon shrugged. I wondered what he was thinking. His family situation was so different from ours it was hard to put yourself in his place.

I got up. "Anybody for ice cream?" I asked.

Simon glanced at his watch. "I hate to leave you two stuck with the telephone, but I've got to go."

I had no doubt that he had a date with Margarita, a standing date, probably, for Saturday night. I sat down again. "Maybe I'll skip the ice cream," I said.

Jack walked Simon out to his car. I stared disconsolately at the telephone. In a few minutes, Jack came back and plopped down beside me. "Boy, is that grim? I can't believe it. Poor Simon. Poor me, for that matter. There isn't a soul in this blinking town to talk to. I'm just going to hate it."

I picked up my empty TV dinner tray and took it to the kitchen. "Maybe I can get Janey to go with me to the television station on Saturdays," I said. "It's more important that you be here to answer the phone. You know just how to handle it."

"That's right! He won't be around to help with the dogs either!" Jack slapped his hand to his brow. "That mother and father of his are something else. Simon's got all his life to learn Spanish, but he's only got one senior year. Is he supposed to go out and spend it with a bunch of perfect strangers."

"He'll make new friends," I said, choking up. "Look, can you take care of the phone? I think I want to go take an aspirin and lie down for a while."

If I felt better later, maybe I would clean my guinea pig's cage.

10

The week after Simon told us he was leaving was one of the strangest I can remember. The strangeness began with Dad calling me from his office Monday afternoon, sounding worried.

"Brenna," he said, "you haven't been in any difficulties your mother and I don't know about have you?"

"What do you mean?"

"Oh, pushing people down on the playground or what have you."

"Dad, it's been a while since I pushed anyone down on the playground," I said patiently. "I'm sixteen years old."

That provoked a moment of silence as Dad was no doubt thinking of how much more trouble you can get into at sixteen than you can when you're on the playground.

"I don't know what is going on," he said finally. "I've been closeted with witnesses all day about this Collins custody case and I come out to find a message from Larry Weatherby asking me to bring you to his office this evening."

Mr. Weatherby is a very stuffy old lawyer. I couldn't figure out why he would want to see me. I scarcely knew him.

"Maybe there's been a mix up about the name?" I suggested.

"Well, he did call my office. He obviously must be clear about who you are," Dad pointed out.

"Didn't Dinah ask what it was about?"

"You will recall Dinah is on vacation," Dad said with controlled emotion, "and the nitwit temporary has the brains of a mollusk. I've tried to call Weatherby back, but he's in court all day, and I've got to get back to this Collins mess myself. Now listen. I'm not sure I'm going to be able to get out of here at six. This case comes up tomorrow and I may be here until midnight. You call your mother and tell her to plan to take you to Weatherby's office tonight. If I can get away, I'll meet you there. Let's find out what's going on so we can all sleep tonight." He muttered something under his breath.

"I haven't been up to anything!" I squeeked.

But after I hung up, of course, I began searching my conscience. One thing about being an attorney's daughter: You have a large, though foggy, idea of all the things that you can do wrong. I searched my mind. Had I done *anything* I might be legally liable for? Had anyone broken a leg tripping over me, or slipped in a puddle I had failed to mop up? Had I knowingly put a vicious dog up for adoption? I thought uneasily of Wolf Dog but discarded the notion. He was just a little spirited, not vicious. On the other hand, could I have unwittingly been a witness to someone else's misdeeds? I couldn't remember any crashing cars or accidents in my vicinity. Of course, the wheels of the law grind exceedingly slow; it could have happened years ago.

Fortunately, Mom didn't take the same pessimistic view of the summons that Dad did. "There's no point in borrowing trouble," she said. "Don't worry yourself sick about this. Go read a book or something. It certainly is provoking that we can't find out what it's about, but we'll just have to put up with it."

It seemed forever until six o'clock. But at last Mom and I arrived at Mr. Weatherby's office, an affair of glass and brick considerably more modern than Mr. Weatherby himself. As we were about to walk in, Dad's car pulled up, so we waited on the sidewalk for him and all went in together.

Mr. Weatherby came out into the waiting room to meet us and shook hands with Daddy. "Good evening, George," he said, "and Mrs. Matthews.

Goodness, young lady, how you have grown! Why the last time I saw you you were in rompers."

This was not strictly true as I had seen him at the Oakdale Fourth of July picnic only a couple of years ago. It was just the sort of conventional remark people like Mr. Weatherby make. At the picnic he had said, "Hot enough for you?" There were no surprises in the conversation of Mr. Weatherby. That is, not until later.

"Have a seat, ladies," he said. "As I told your secretary, George, I called you all here tonight to apprise you of the provisions of a trust set up by Miss Letitia Talmidge."

That certainly explained why the temporary hadn't gotten the message. Doubtless she hadn't an idea what "provision" and "trust" meant, much less "apprise." I grasped the gist of what he was saying, but I was still confused. I had never heard of Letitia Talmidge.

Dad immediately relaxed since this opening remark made it unlikely Mr. Weatherby's next words would be "criminal liability."

Mr. Weatherby put on his glasses and peered at his notes.

"But we don't know any Letitia Talmidge," I said.

He peered over his glasses at me and smiled. "Ah, but she knows you. And thinks very highly of the work you are doing with Oakdale's stray dogs. Now Miss Talmidge has set up a substantial trust for the work of the Dog Protection Society.

It is her wish that the society have a modest building with kennels in which to house the dogs and that it be able to employ a full-time attendant to care for the dogs and show them to prospective owners. The monies for this will come from the income of the trust. At such time as the Dog Protection Society should become defunct, the capital as well as the properties, the kennels and grounds, will revert to the estate of Miss Talmidge and to charities she has designated. If at any time the income of the trust proves inadequate to sustain the society, the trustees are empowered to draw on the capital of the trust until it is depleted, as long as the society continues its work to the satisfaction of the trustees. The trustees named by Miss Talmidge are myself, the Oakdale Farmer's Bank, and Miss Brenna Matthews."

Dad was leaning back in his chair in amazement. "But the trust must be for a very large amount of money," he said. "What prompted Miss Talmidge to do this? Brenna says she doesn't even know the woman."

Mr. Weatherby tapped his fingertips together. "As Miss Talmidge said to me so colorfully on the occasion of drawing up the trust, 'You never see a hearse pulling a U-Haul-It.'" He looked back at his notes. "Miss Talmidge has determined to her satisfaction that this is the best way of expressing her lifelong affection for animals."

I was simply flabbergasted. It was hard to take it all in. "Wait a minute," I said, suddenly seeing light. "Is Miss Talmidge a little old lady with white hair in a hair net and black lace-up shoes?"

"Miss Talmidge is elderly," assented Mr. Weatherby, "and conservative in her dress. She normally resides in Massachusetts, but while visiting a friend in Raleigh, she saw the Dog Protection Society's television advertisement and began to investigate its activities. She was impressed by the integrity with which the operations were conducted." A surprising glint of humor appeared in Mr. Weatherby's eye. "I feel," he added, "that Miss Talmidge may have been somewhat influenced in her decision by the desire to disappoint an impecunious nephew who has taken to hanging around her in perhaps a tactlessly expectant way. Be that as it may, I think we should begin at once planning for the future of the Dog Protection Society. I am leaving on vacation tomorrow and wanted to lay this before you before I left so you could be thinking about what would be best. When I return we will need to begin planning the activities of the trust. We'll need blueprints and bids from builders. We'll want to interview prospective employees, that sort of thing. Perhaps you could study the layouts of typical kennels in the weeks to come and get some idea of what would be desirable."

I walked out of Mr. Weatherby's office in a daze. It was hard to take it all in. We would be able to have a real building and someone to answer the phone and show the dogs.

Dad sped back to his office and the Collins case, happy that another day had passed without bringing disaster to his family.

"You don't seem exactly bubbling over with happiness," Mom commented as we drove home.

"It's all so new," I said. "I'll have to get used to it. There will be a whole new bunch of things to worry about—getting someone really reliable to work for us, getting the building built." I paused a moment then blurted out, "And where do *I* fit in? If we are able to find someone really good to take care of the dogs and show them, what is there for me to do?"

"I have a feeling there'll be plenty for you to do," said Mom. "After all, you know you couldn't have gone on doing all this forever. School will be starting, and eventually you'll be going away to college."

I slumped a bit in the seat. "I know. You're right. The trust fund is really terrific and I should be awfully glad. But I don't know. I feel sort of . . . let down. Up to now, the society has been my very own thing and it's been nice to feel . . . so important . . . as if so much depended on me."

"Well, don't be determined to wring all the misery you can out of this piece of luck," said Mother wryly.

Jack was tremendously excited when we told him the news. "Let's go tell Si," he said. "I can't wait to see his face!"

I murmured something about calling first. I

wasn't keen about the possibility of catching Margarita there, but Jack wouldn't hear of calling. So in moments we were at Simon's and at last I could feel myself getting caught up in the excitement of it all. It was really the most tremendous piece of good luck. When I started thinking of it, we could do the job so much better with the proper facilities. We had been saying all along that it would be so much better if we had a single central location with all the dogs there for people to choose from. It was bound to speed up the adoption process.

Simon was jubilant. "I can't believe it! This is really the answer to all our problems! You must have made one heck of an impression on Miss Talmidge, Brenna. Let's celebrate," he said expansively. "Have you two had dinner?"

We talked it over and decided to do something more special than pizza or hamburgers.

"We'll have to stop by the house for money," I said.

"My treat," said Simon. "This is my birthday and Dad sent me some money."

"Your birthday!" I said in dismay. "Why didn't you tell us it was your birthday! We could have baked a cake."

"I didn't mention it was my birthday because I didn't feel like celebrating," said Simon lightly, "but now I do."

After calling to check in with Mom, we ended up at Trianon House because it's a place where you don't have to really dress up, but it's nice. I mean, it's not one of those places with big stacks of baby high chairs at the entrance and with restroom doors labeled "Cowgirls" and "Bucka-roos."

The sun was sifting hazily through the thin draperies as we walked into the dining room. White tablecloths hung in heavy folds from the tables and there was a gleam of candles.

"I love fresh strawberries," said Jack, greedily eyeing the silver bowl full of them at the buffet. "I think we came to the right place."

Fortunately, the place really began to fill up as soon as we got our order in, so you didn't have to speak in whispers.

"Aren't you excited about all this, Brenna, honestly?" asked Simon, lifting a forkful of fish. "Think of it, a building of our own, no more begging people to board dogs, really good facilities for a change."

"It will be awfully nice," I said. "I have to admit I used to worry a lot about what would happen to the society when we three couldn't do all the work anymore."

"What we need to do next," said Jack, "is try to decide exactly what we need. It'll be too late to make changes after the building is up."

"Maybe Brenna and I could go around and look at some kennels and some other dog shel-ters, that kind of thing. Find out what works out," said Simon.

Jack and I averted our eyes. We were both thinking that Simon might be gone before this extensive research project could be begun. It was like when you're with someone who isn't expected to live out the year. Everyone studiously avoids mentioning what is on everybody's mind.

In spite of this black cloud, which seemed at times to hover just over Simon's arched eyebrows and at other times to drift out of sight towards the dining room chandelier, we had a very nice celebration. Out of the kindness of our hearts, Jack and I agreed not to sing "Happy Birthday" to Simon, and the food was very good. Trianon House's fresh seafood is justly renowned.

The stars had come out by the time we made our way through the parking lot back to Simon's car. As we walked in that direction, Simon put his arm around me. I almost stumbled in my astonishment. Fleetingly I wondered if Margarita would have been jealous if she could have seen us walking arm in arm. Then I decided morosely that someone as sophisticated as Margarita could probably recognize a show of brotherly affection when she saw it. Still, I savored the warmth of his arm around me. Particularly since it was probably the first and last time this would ever happen.

Jack, of course, averted his eyes. Considering the way everybody was determinedly averting his eyes that evening, it was amazing no one tripped and broke a toe.

11

The rest of the week was, if anything, stranger than its beginning. Even Jack had noticed that Simon was getting more and more tense.

"Simon would get along better," Jack said bluntly, "if he talked about what was on his mind."

"Simon has had more to worry him than you two have," said Mom. "You can't expect him to have the same devil-may-care manner."

"You know what I mean, don't you?" Jack asked me.

Actually, I did know what he meant. Simon did

talk about what was on his mind, but not in casual driblets the way most people do. He was the sort of person who would go all week worrying about something and you wouldn't find out what it was until he burst out with it on Saturday.

"He has a habit of secrecy," said Jack firmly.

"He's probably had to learn to keep his own counsel," said Mom, which is the same thing but in nicer words.

Mom seemed to imagine Jack was criticizing Simon, but I could tell he was just worried about him. It might be boring when people prattle on about how they can't stand their Aunt Nancy and how they nearly died trying to decide which shoes to buy, but I guess it does let off tension. With Simon, when something was on his mind, his eyes just got darker and he got quieter. Ever since the big celebration about the new trust fund, that's the way he had been. Jack and I knew he was upset about having to move away, but he didn't seem to want to complain about it, which was weird in itself.

Jack appealed to me. "You know what I mean, don't you, Brenna? We've never finished last week's chess game, so I said 'Come on over tonight.' He said he couldn't. Well, you see what I mean. Most people would give you some reason why they couldn't. But not Simon. You'd think he was working for the CIA, not talking to his best friend."

Jack had to get off to work, so the discussion of

Simon's character ended there, but after what Jack had said, I was a little surprised when Simon called that afternoon at five-thirty.

"Jack's not in yet," I said. "He's having to work late."

"I don't want to talk to Jack," he said. "I want to talk to you. Why don't I pick you up in a few minutes and we'll go get a hamburger?"

"That was Simon," I said to Mom after I hung up. "He wants to go out and get hamburgers. Is that okay?"

"Sure."

"Don't you think it's odd his calling me like this?"

"Not particularly," said Mom.

"But he just told Jack he was tied up tonight, now suddenly it seems he's not. I wonder what he wants to talk about."

When I thought about it, I figured he must have some idea about the future construction of the dog shelter. I remembered how he hadn't spilled the news about the television spot until it was all settled. Maybe he had been out all day studying kennels, had gotten home earlier than he thought, and now I was going to hear about his great new plan.

In a matter of minutes, Simon was at the kitchen door.

"Hi, Mrs. Matthews. Ready, Brenna?"

Something was definitely up. Simon was holding on to the kitchen doorknob as if he were trying to anchor himself in a hurricane and was positively taut with suppressed news.

I gave Mom a quick good-bye and headed out to the car. No sooner had we closed the door to the car than Simon let out a wild Indian war whoop. I saw Mom's face bob up in alarm at the kitchen window. I jumped myself, but I gave her a reassuring wave. Simon was showing signs of insanity, but did not as yet look dangerous.

"No Dominican Republic!" he said, stepping smartly on the accelerator.

The red car zipped down our street. I melted weakly into the seat cushions. "What happened?" I asked.

"It's a long story," he said, with the familiar little lordly wave. It warmed my heart to see traces of the old arrogance returning, apparently in good repair. There hadn't been much sign of it lately.

"Tell me anyway," I said. "Start at the beginning."

He grinned at me. "Well, I met Dad in Raleigh for lunch. He was stopping over on business and asked me to drive down so we could have lunch together. The idea was that he might stay a couple of days, but he got his business wound up faster than he thought and left this afternoon. I met him at the St. Regis." Simon's eyebrows drew lower. "I had been thinking for weeks about what I was going to say, but when I first saw him I nearly lost my nerve. I decided just to charge ahead and not think, so as soon as we sat down I blurted out that I didn't want to go to the Dominican Republic. Then I concentrated on my menu and tried to look confident. So then he said, 'There's a girl behind this isn't there?'"

My heart sank. Margarita again. Simon's father, in spite of his manifold faults, seemed to have the gift of second sight.

"I said that was part of it," Simon went on, "but not the only thing. 'It's my life,' I said, 'and anyway I'm not sure I want to be an importer.'" Simon lifted a hand from the steering wheel to rub his nose. "Actually, that's not true," he admitted. "If Dad were to sell the business I'd howl like a banshee, but I got a little carried away."

"What did he say when you said that?"

"Actually, what he said doesn't make any sense. You have to have hung around my mother and father as long as I have to see the crazy logic of it. He said, 'You know, I didn't want the divorce.'"

"What?"

"I told you it didn't make any sense, but it's like by crossing him I was getting back at him for the divorce, you see? So when he said that I nearly threw up my hand and said 'Oh, I'll go. Forget it. That's all right.'"

"I don't think I quite grasp this," I said. Say what you will about my family, what they said usually made sense and what they said was also usually what they meant. I hadn't had much practice at sorting out conversations like they had in Simon's family.

"I just get to feeling so guilty," Simon explained, "when he gets like that. But this time I stood my ground. I said it didn't have anything to do with him and Mother. I just wanted to go to school in the U.S. Not just high school, but college, too." Simon exhaled heavily. "You see," he explained, "I've been thinking about it and thinking about it, worrying about what to say to him for weeks, and I had made up my mind. I figured I just had to take the position that Dad isn't going to curl up and die if I don't always do just what he wants."

It's funny how things work out. I had figured that Simon was afraid of his father, but it turns out he's afraid *for* him. I suppose, when I think about it, that underneath, a lot of dictator types are kind of pathetic.

We pulled up at the McDonald's parking lot, but we didn't get out of the car.

"So what happened then?" I asked.

"So then he dropped his napkin. He bent over to get it and then he straightened up, all red-faced, and said actually he had been going to tell me that they were having labor troubles at the plant—violence and all—and this wasn't a good time for me to go anyway."

"What a coincidence!"

Simon shrugged. "That's just Dad for you."

"You mean you don't think it's true?"

"I expect it's true, all right, as far as it goes. I

expect they are having troubles at the plant, but I doubt it had occurred to him until just then that there was a reason for me not to go. It's just hard for him to back down. He needs to save face. So then he said, 'I want for you to be happy.'" Simon sighed. "And he does, too."

If his father wanted him to be happy, it seemed to me he didn't go about it in a very efficient way, but I said warmly, "That's terrific, Simon. It really is. Jack is going to be so happy."

He gave me a funny look. "Aren't you happy, too?"

"Oh, yes," I said. "I'm really happy for you. It's wonderful!"

He reached over and brushed my ear with his fingertips. "Good," he said, "because I've got a month of summer left, and I'm looking forward, now, to spending it with you."

Then he kissed me. Right there in the McDonald's parking lot. Of course, a truly sensible person would have just enjoyed it. But my problem is that I can't seem to turn my mind off. As soon as I caught my breath I said, "But what about Margarita?"

Simon pulled away and looked puzzled. "Oh, I'll go on with my Spanish lessons. Dad's right. I really need the Spanish."

"But I thought you and Margarita were . . . I mean, you were at that play together."

"Sure. It was a good play for both of us. I've been reading it in Spanish with Professor Posada and seeing the English version was a help to me.

Then Margarita knows the Spanish version so seeing it in English helps her with English. See?"

I saw. I wondered if what had transpired in the Japanese garden had left Margarita bitterly disappointed. I looked at Simon and saw that he was laughing at me.

"Good grief, Brenna," he said. "Margarita is a cat person."

Then he kissed me again. Oakdale streamed by the car on its way in to get hamburgers, no doubt all of them taking notes for the grapevine. Then Simon said he was hungry. Personally, I felt like I'd never eat again, but we went in and ordered.

Once we were settled in a yellow booth, Simon bit robustly into his cheeseburger and said, "I feel so great it makes me realize how awful I've felt for weeks." He put his arm around me and squeezed me close. "With all that hanging over me . . ." He didn't have to finish the sentence. I knew him well enough to finish it in my mind. Simon, who couldn't stop himself from thinking ahead, wouldn't start a romance he wasn't going to be around to conduct properly. That was what had really been going on. Not Margarita at all.

It was the nicest supper I had ever had at McDonald's. I kept experiencing the most fascinating sensations. My heart was leaping quite strangely, as if little strings in it were going "ping." When we walked out to the car the pavement wouldn't stay beneath my feet—I seemed to be floating. I felt as if I could have danced all night. Really, it was like a medley of top pop hits of the past. It made me wonder if the truth in life is to be found, after all, in clichés—in which case I guess old Mr. Weatherby has achieved the highest reaches of wisdom.

Jack's jalopy was in the driveway when we got in, and Simon came in to tell him the good news himself. Jack pounded him on the back in this insane way guys have while I danced my way into the family room. "Simon's not leaving," I sang. "He's staying here." Simon and Jack followed me in to where Mom and Dad were.

"Congratulations, Simon," Dad said. "We would have been sorry to lose you."

Simon put his arm around me and gave me a peck on the forehead. "I would have been even sorrier to go," he said.

"Let's break out the champagne," said Mom. She groped around in the refrigerator and, to my surprise, pulled out a bottle of real champagne from behind a couple of heads of leaf lettuce. "I was saving it to celebrate the end of that horrible Collins custody case," she said, "but this is better." Then, corkscrew in hand, she peered at the safety warnings. Mine must be the only mother in the country who reads out loud the safety warnings on a bottle of champagne. "Let's see, 'Point away from yourself and others. Open slowly.'" Finally, she managed to extricate the cork with a quiet, safe little pop and Dad poured champagne all around.

It's at times like this that I realize that Mom and Dad really love us. They like to have Simon around, but it wasn't on that account that they were beaming. It was because they wanted us to be happy.

Simon had to get home because his mother was about to get in from class and he was anxious to tell her the news. When Simon turned to leave, that was when I realized that even Jack loves me, because he headed towards the door, then he suddenly thought twice, pulled up short, and let me walk Simon out to the car alone.

It would have suited me better if we had walked out into velvety night and stars, but instead the summer sky was still hot and bright and five neighbors had perfect visibility of Simon's car in front of our house. When you live in a small town, you have to learn to adapt. I brushed a bit of lint off his shirt and looked discreet volumes with my eyes. Simon, however, blew my cover. He unceremoniously picked me up, put me on the fender of the car, and kissed my hand. When I slid down, blushing, he kissed me again. "People are looking," I hissed. Simon's eyebrows went up. "Should I wave?" You could tell that Simon was not brought up in a small town, and from the looks of it, he might never get the hang of it. But maybe that wasn't all bad, I thought.

12

A couple of days later, Janey dropped by the house. I could see that if she kept up at this rate with the sailing, she was going to end up with cordovan-colored skin.

"I hear you and Simon are now an item," she said. "I thought you were just good friends."

"We're still good friends," I said. "We're just better friends than I thought." I settled into a chair with a satisfied sigh. "Where did you hear all this? I just found out myself."

"Oh, Suzy Lampton called me up on purpose last night to see if I knew. Of course, I said I did.

Then Mrs. Marriville told Mamma she had witnessed a shocking exhibition outside your house night before last. Mamma immediately concluded the neighbors had rioted on account of the dogs howling and was very disappointed to learn she was just talking about kissing. Oh, and I forgot to mention that Suzy says Olivia Dawes is livid because she is taking physics next year purely in order to be in the same class with Simon and now it's too late for her to get out."

"Sometimes I think I'd like to live in New York City or London or Moscow," I said wildly, "one of those places where nobody cares whether you live or die."

"You know you'd miss Oakdale," said Janey placidly. She produced an embroidery hoop and began to do cross-stitch with brown thread. I peered at it but couldn't quite make out the pattern. "It's going to be a portrait of my dog," she explained. "I'm going to do his name—Squiggles—across the bottom in satin stitch, then when it's finished I'm going to make it into a pillow."

A dog pillow—Janey might not have much taste, but you had to give her credit for being a first class animal lover.

"How are the plans for the dog shelter coming?" she asked.

"I think they're firming up at last," I said. "We're starting construction next week and the contractor promises we can move in by October first."

"Figure by Christmas," said Janey cynically, snipping a thread with her teeth.

She was wrong though. By Halloween we had moved the Dog Protection Society bag and baggage into the new building. We wanted Miss Talmidge to come down for the dedication, but she passed it up. It turns out she follows the sun, and Halloween is the date of her annual move from New England to the Bahamas. The dedication was a festive occasion, nevertheless. Our new shelter was no architectural achievement, just a basic, stripped-down cement block building, but it looked very cheerful, the doors and windows decorated with balloons and streamers bobbing around in the autumn wind. We had an open house for the town with cookies and punch. The road's edge and the driveway were jammed with cars of people coming to look us over.

Sergeant Mulhoney was there, of course, I found him sitting near the dipping pit, balancing a paper plate stacked with cookies. "This is a great day for Oakdale," he intoned, gesturing broadly with a cookie. "Not to mention for me," he confided. "I had my application for the highway patrol pulled this morning. I can see now that this shelter thing of yours is really going to work. What a relief! The trouble with the highway patrol," he said, lowering his voice, "is that when you pull over a car, you never know when there might be a criminal in it." He bit into another cookie. Sometimes I wondered if Sergeant Mulhoney had gone into the right field of work.

Dr. Briggs stopped in for a moment, too. Making his way through the crush in the little reception room, he almost knocked over the potted chrysanthemums the chamber of commerce had sent us in honor of our official opening. I moved the flowers to the back of the reception desk for safe keeping. "I've got to be getting back to the office," he said, "but I wanted to pop in and take a look. This is quite a setup you have here."

I looked suitably modest. "We had to stay within a budget," I said, "but we were able to put in most of the things we wanted. And it's set up so we can expand later if we need to."

Simon made his way through the crowd bearing two additional plates of cookies. Jack followed with three cans of punch. We had had a bigger crowd show up than we expected. We hadn't taken into account how little there is to do on a Sunday afternoon in Oakdale. A tour of the Dog Protection Society's new building turned out to be the top-ranking entertainment of the day.

"I wonder when all these people are going to take off," Simon muttered to me. "We said two to four o'clock and it's four now. They're still all over the place. I just had to get some man out of the bathroom when the lock jammed."

"Oh, dear," I said. "What if someone else gets stuck in there?"

"Don't worry," said Simon. "I put an 'Out of order' sign up."

"Well, that's one comfort," said Jack. "They

can't stay here indefinitely if the bathroom is out of order."

"What we need," I said, "is some way to wind up this open house."

Jack's eyes took on a cunning look. "I've got it. Have no fear. I'll take care of it."

He disappeared from my sight for a minute, but then I could see him standing up on a chair by the window. "The final tour of the building is now beginning," he shouted. "Gather here for the final tour of the building." Sheeplike, people all over the room dropped their cookies and gathered around him. "Right this way!" he barked. "Follow me." Slowly the crowd squeezed its way through the door to the hall. I could hear their progress as they made their way at a brisk trot through the grooming room, along the runs, past the bathroom, through the isolation room and out the back door. The dogs went wild barking.

"Follow them," ordered Simon. "Lock the back door behind them!"

Obediently, I dashed through the building and locked the door behind the last guest. I just hoped there were no stragglers locked in the bathroom or anything. When I got back to the reception room, Simon was turning off the lights. "Turning the lights out," he said, "will be a little hint that the open house is now closed." I heard a timid knock on the front door and opened it. "I'm afraid I left my purse," said a middle-aged woman. While I helped her find her purse, some more people came back for their coats, but the dim lights seemed to do the trick, and cars were already pulling out of the driveway. I gathered up the empty cookie plates and punch cans while Simon swept the cigarette butts off the floor.

"People are such slobs," he said.

"We should have put out ash trays," I said.

Jack appeared to collect congratulations on his strategy. "It worked!" he crowed. "Didn't it?"

"It's a good thing it did," I said, hoisting a bag of trash to carry to the car. "I've got to get home. I have an *awful* lot of homework to get done."

I had followed Dr. Briggs' advice and beefed up my academic schedule. It hurt, but I dropped off the yearbook staff and out of chorus to gain two hours for trig and physics. At first it looked like I wasn't going to be able to get into physics at the last minute because it was full, but Olivia Dawes was keen to get out of it, so they let me take her place.

I found physics pretty tough slugging. I am not the sort of person who when left in a room with a lamp and a notebook automatically comes out having discovered the theory of relativity. In fact, now that I was struggling with physics, I deeply regretted that I had let my brain go flabby during biology by always volunteering to be the one who took the notes when the frog was dissected.

As for trig, the first week it looked like I was going to have to develop a close personal relationship with a tutor. I had more than a bit of catching up to do. Fortunately, after the first few weeks I began to see light, though. I wasn't even that bad at physics and trig. It was just that at first it was a bit of a shock to realize how much I was going to have to work.

Meanwhile, poor Jack was up to his neck in decisions about college. In November, Dad took a week off from work to take him on a tour of some possible colleges so he could get the feel of various campuses, but in spite of Dad's efforts, Jack was fast being driven crazy trying to distinguish between the schools. The night they got back, I could hear Dad reaching his breaking point in the family room. "What on earth does it matter whether or not they offer roller skating?" he said in tones of controlled fury. "And I do not feel its nearness to Mardi Gras should be a factor in your decision."

Later I overheard Dad saying to Mom in sad tones, "Ellie, I don't know why I never noticed it before, but Jack needs a sense of direction in his life." I stifled a laugh. Jack had all my sympathy, but it was bliss to have the heat on someone else for a change.

Leaving everyone agonizing about Jack's future, I went to bed early. The next day was a teacher-planning day, a school holiday, and I for one needed a holiday. It wasn't just my school work. Part of what kept me so busy was the shelter. Mona, the girl we hired to work at the shelter, was devoted to the dogs, a real jewel. But there were lots of decisions she couldn't make on her own. We always had to be conferring. Furthermore, any special expenditure, like the time it

turned out we had to regrade the shelter grounds
to avoid flooding, required my meeting with Mr.
Weatherby and a bank officer. Mom certainly had
been right about how hard it would have been to
keep the Dog Protection Society going single-
handedly once school started. Even with Mona's
help I was pedaling hard to keep up. The other
thing that filled up my schedule—and I'm not
complaining about it for a minute—was Simon.
When they had the Autumn Stomp, the bonfire,
the Homecoming Dance, the Halloween Carnival
—Simon and I were there. On top of that, we
spent a fair amount of time together just talking,
walking, and kicking the leaves around. I had to
work hard to fit in all that fun. I sometimes
thought it was one of life's little ironies that the
fun, fun time I had planned had not materialized
in the summer when I had the time for it, but in
the fall when I was coping with physics and trig.
Of course, I didn't mind. I was very happy and I
wouldn't have changed a single thing about my
life. It was just that sometimes I was overcome by
this deep and profound desire to sleep a long,
long time. So you can be sure that when a school
holiday turned up, the first thing I was going to do
was to sack out.

It was ten the next morning when I finally got
out of bed. I walked somnolently through the
living room, my eyes protesting the buttery sunshine streaming in through the front windows,
thinking that maybe after breakfast I might take
just a bit of a nap. As I passed him, I saw that

Jack was sitting beside the chessboard making notations on a piece of graph paper.

"What's up?" I yawned.

He shot me a black glance. "I'm going over to Simon's. While I'm at it, I'm going to transfer this game to his board."

I saw now that he was making a diagram of the positions of all the chess pieces.

"Why can't Simon just come over here?" I asked.

Jack didn't answer but, tight-lipped, jotted down the position of Simon's bishop. I tied the sash of my bathrobe so I wouldn't trip on it, and continued my progress to the kitchen, thoughtfully. I may be a little slow when I first get up, but eventually I catch on. Obviously Jack wanted to go over to Simon's so he could pour out his troubles in complete privacy.

A few minutes later, when I was cracking an egg into the frying pan, I heard Jack's jalopy backfiring on its way out the driveway. I grinned. It was all right with me if Jack felt he needed some time with Simon when I wasn't hanging about. There was enough of Simon to go around.

After that, Simon and Jack made a practice of playing their chess games in Simon's living room and everybody was happy.

There was one thing that never changed, though. Summer or fall, whatever else was going on, Saturday mornings always found Simon and me driving to the television station with three dogs in tow. One week I tried to get Mona to go with us. "Someday you'll probably have to do this by yourself, Mona," I said. "Oh, no, I couldn't!" she said, her teeth chattering.

"There just wasn't a thing I could do to persuade her to come along," I told Simon later as we drove to the station.

"I wouldn't mention it to her again," he said. "You can see it upsets her and you don't want Mona to start looking for another job."

The idea of it shot a thrill of fear through me. "Goodness no. Oh, I promise I won't mention it again!" I said nervously. "But it's true Simon. She will have to do it eventually, once I leave for college."

"You don't even know Mona will still be working for the shelter by then. Why should she stay forever in a job with no advancement, no pension plan, no fringe benefits."

"Because she likes dogs?"

But I could see that Simon had a point. The job at the shelter, at what we were able to pay, was more a beginning-type job. I had to expect there was going to be some turnover. This habit of Simon's of looking ahead could be unnerving. He had given me something else to worry about.

A worrier, I learned, will always find something to worry about. Back in the summer I had worried that Simon would never be more to me than Jack's best friend. Now that he and I seemed so close, I worried about all the glamorous women he would be meeting when he went away to school. I managed to work myself up into quite a state about that one day. Foolishly, I imagined that Janey would be a great comfort to me because she was going through the same thing. Gary would be attending State next fall, planning eventually to specialize in actuarial science, a discipline that seemed made to order for him. When I went over to Janey's however, she wasn't exactly the comfort I had hoped.

"It's fatal to be possessive," said Janey loftily. "I've been careful never to put the slightest pressure on Gary to go to school near home and I *never* ask him if he thinks he'll be able to get home weekends."

"But you've known all along that Gary is going to State," I protested. "And it's only an hour's drive away."

"The principle is the same. I don't want Gary to feel tied down."

"That's really noble of you, Janey."

"It's just practical. After all, I don't want to be tied down either. Next year, *I'll* be the one getting ready to go away," her eyes began to gleam, "and meet all sorts of glamorous college men."

My heart sank. Janey didn't seem to realize that, in these days of coeducation, where there were glamorous men there were likely to be an equal number of glamorous college women.

However, I realized that basically Janey was right. No one could tell what was over the horizon for us all. When people left home and went away to school, things sometimes changed a lot. I still remembered Nadine Hodfelter, who had left home a cheerleader and come back a Buddhist monk. Not that I could imagine Simon as a Buddhist monk, but it just showed there was no point in worrying about tomorrow because you can never really know what is going to happen. For example, it wouldn't have occurred to me last spring that I would be so happy working myself silly. I guess I have more of my parents in me than I thought. All along I must have been a budding workaholic without realizing it.

Reflecting on these things, I decided to try very hard just to appreciate the good times I was having in the here and now. That was what Simon said he was doing. He said he'd become a complete convert to my philosophy and intended to gather his rosebuds while he might. I should add that it was easy for him since he breezed through his homework in no time. He imagined that I found it just as easy to get everything done. For instance, doing the television spot put a big hole in Saturday, but that never deterred Simon from making plans for us to do something together Saturday night. "Just get that English paper done Friday night," he said. "Then we can go to the dance Saturday night and you'll still have Sunday to work on the trig." It all sounded very plausible. It was only after he hung up that I remembered I was going to have to do things like wash and blow dry my hair and clean my room sometime or other.

"Efficiency," Mom reassured me. "The key is efficiency, dear." And I guess it must have been because by late Saturday afternoon my English paper was written, my room clean, and by seven-fifteen, my scalp still tingling from the blow drier, I was pinning flowers in my hair. At seven-thirty, right on schedule, I was getting into Simon's car.

"I can't get over it," he said, looking up at the sky as he opened my door. "It's such a beautiful night." The stars were burning with that clear, cold light you get on still autumn evenings. He walked around to his side of the car and slid in. "Beautiful night, beautiful girl," he grinned. It was going to be very hard, I thought, to get used to the flat manner of the typical Oakdale boy after going with Simon.

"I've applied to Duke," Simon announced as he backed slowly out of the driveway, taking care not to scatter the gravel. "It's a good school," he said, "and I think I'll get in."

My heart gave one of those strange little pings. Duke isn't but an hour and a half's drive away.

"I've decided," he said simply, "that I don't want to go very far away."

I couldn't tell you what the decorations were like or exactly who was there, but it was a perfectly wonderful dance. And after all, I can always catch up on my sleep some other year.

Four exciting First Love from Silhouette romances yours for 15 days—_free!_

If you enjoyed this First Love from Silhouette® you'll want to read more! These are true-to-life romances about the things that matter most to you now—your friendships, dating, getting along in school, and learning about yourself. The stories could really happen, and the characters are so real they'll seem like friends.

Now you can get 4 First Love from Silhouette romances to look over for 15 days—absolutely free! If you decide not to keep them, simply return them and pay nothing. But if you enjoy them as much as we believe you will, keep them and pay the invoice enclosed with your trial shipment. You'll then become a member of the First Love from Silhouette℠ Book Club and will receive 4 more new First Love from Silhouette romances every month. You'll always be among the first to get them, and you'll never miss a new title. There is no minimum number of books to buy and you can cancel at any time. To receive your 4 books, mail the coupon below today.

First Love from Silhouette® is a service mark and a registered trademark of Simon & Schuster.

First Love from Silhouette

THERE'S NOTHING QUITE AS SPECIAL AS A FIRST LOVE.

$1.75 each

2 ☐ GIRL IN THE ROUGH Wunsch

3 ☐ PLEASE LET ME IN Beckman

4 ☐ SERENADE Marceau

6 ☐ KATE HERSELF Erskine

7 ☐ SONGBIRD Enfield

14 ☐ PROMISED KISS Ladd

15 ☐ SUMMER ROMANCE Diamond

16 ☐ SOMEONE TO LOVE Bryan

17 ☐ GOLDEN GIRL Erskine

18 ☐ WE BELONG TOGETHER Harper

19 ☐ TOMORROW'S WISH Ryan

20 ☐ SAY PLEASE! Francis

$1.95

24 ☐ DREAM LOVER Treadwell

26 ☐ A TIME FOR US Ryan

27 ☐ A SECRET PLACE Francis

29 ☐ FOR THE LOVE OF LORI Ladd

30 ☐ A BOY TO DREAM ABOUT Quinn

31 ☐ THE FIRST ACT London

32 ☐ DARE TO LOVE Bush

33 ☐ YOU AND ME Johnson

34 ☐ THE PERFECT FIGURE March

35 ☐ PEOPLE LIKE US Haynes

36 ☐ ONE ON ONE Ketter

37 ☐ LOVE NOTE Howell

38 ☐ ALL-AMERICAN GIRL Payton

39 ☐ BE MY VALENTINE Harper

40 ☐ MY LUCKY STAR Cassiday

41 ☐ JUST FRIENDS Francis

42 ☐ PROMISES TO COME Dellin

43 ☐ A KNIGHT TO REMEMBER Martin

44 ☐ SOMEONE LIKE JEREMY VAUGHN Alexander

45 ☐ A TOUCH OF LOVE Madison

46 ☐ SEALED WITH A KISS Davis

47 ☐ THREE WEEKS OF LOVE Aks

48 ☐ SUMMER ILLUSION Manning

49 ☐ ONE OF A KIND Brett

50 ☐ STAY, SWEET LOVE Fisher

51 ☐ PRAIRIE GIRL Coy

52 ☐ A SUMMER TO REMEMBER Robertson

First Love from Silhouette

Coming in December . . .
NEED A GOOD LAUGH? read
SEND IN THE CLOWNS
by Marilyn Youngblood

FIRST LOVE, Department FL/4
1230 Avenue of the Americas
New York, NY 10020

Please send me the books I have checked above. I am enclosing
$_____ (please add 75¢ to cover postage and handling. NYS and
NYC residents please add appropriate sales tax). Send check
or money order—no cash or C.O.D.'s please. Allow six weeks for
delivery.

NAME _____

ADDRESS _____

CITY _____ STATE/ZIP _____

Coming Next Month

Advice And Consent by Bea Alexander

Lori was Ms. Lonely hearts of Lincoln High. All her classmates came to her for guidance and counsel. How come she could straighten out every one else's love life but not her own?

More Than Friends by Becky Stuart

They came from different worlds. Neal was the richest girl in town. Rick was a poor boy who worked in her father's garage. How could he ever tell her that more than anything he had ever wanted in his life, he wanted to be more than a friend to her?

That Certain Boy by Doreen Owens Malek

When Gaby first fell in love with Heath it was pure happiness. But soon their relationship swept them into deep waters. Could she cope with her new found tumultuous feelings and still be friends with *that certain boy?*

Love And Honors by Oneta Ryan

When Susan heard that she had earned a place in a special program for the gifted, she was horrified. She knew her friends would consider her weird and she worried about keeping up with the work. Before long she found out that she was truly gifted . . . in a new and exciting sense of the word.

Silhouette Romance

15-Day Free Trial Offer
6 Silhouette Romances

6 Silhouette Romances, free for 15 days! We'll send you 6 new Silhouette Romances to keep for 15 days, absolutely free! If you decide not to keep them, send them back to us. You pay nothing.

Free Home Delivery. But if you enjoy them as much as we think you will, keep them by paying the invoice enclosed with your free trial shipment. We'll pay all shipping and handling charges. You get the convenience of Home Delivery and we pay the postage and handling charge each month.

Don't miss a copy. The Silhouette Book Club is the way to make sure you'll be able to receive every new romance we publish before they're sold out. There is no minimum number of books to buy and you can cancel at any time.

This offer expires June 30, 1984

 Silhouette Book Club, Dept. SF2273
120 Brighton Road, Clifton, NJ 07012

Please send me 6 Silhouette Romances to keep for 15 days, absolutely free. I understand I am not obligated to join the Silhouette Book Club unless I decide to keep them.

NAME _____

ADDRESS _____

CITY _____

STATE _____ ZIP _____